DISCARD

THE
CRANES
OF
IBYCUS

THE
CRANES
OF
IBYCUS

Mary Craig

HAWTHORN BOOKS, INC.

Publishers / NEW YORK

All characters in this tale are purely fictitious and any resemblance they might bear to actual persons, living or dead, is purely coincidental.

For
Caroline Barrett,
that the Gods may favor her time

Contents

Part One

The Brothers of Night

Part Two

The Knees of the Gods

Part Three

Shadows on the Opposite Wall

PART ONE

The Brothers
of Night

*Night, having sleep, the brother of death,
from whose eyelids as they looked,
dropped love.*

HESIOD

1

THE NIGHT OF
WAKENING

The search for Mathew Martin began a little before dawn on an undistinguished day of March while the cold ticked in the joints of my grandfather's house and its eaves sang with rivulets of rain.

March the fifteenth, 1972. The papers read just like any other day; the presidential campaigns were grinding into gear, the news from Indochina was mixed, a storm was moving in, and the usual collection of violence—a bank robbery complete with pictures of the robber caught by hidden camera, and an inevitable murder of passion in some obscure town in the West.

There was nothing recorded that related at all to classic tragedies or the ties of the past lacing men to their doom;

it was a simple day in complex times being bled in ink across a mediocre paper.

But with the first word of the search for Mathew Martin, I suppose I should have been able to hear in my subconscious mind the sound of a door closing. I didn't. In fact, only slowly did I even suspect that the search that was requested of me that gray morning would lead me into a labyrinthine maze where I would wander backwards and forwards. And that in time I would arrive at a place from which I would never return to being the plain Chrys Clement that I had been for nineteen years. My childhood would open and close for me like a great transient flower, to become an alien place haunted only by memories.

I wakened, as I have so many nights of my life, to the still darkness of a sleeping house. I have never been a steady sleeper, even as a child, and wakening to the darkness of my grandfather's house was an ordinary and comfortable thing to do.

I was on semester break from college. It was good to be home, to be pampered by his housekeeper, Vinnie, to spend long gentle hours with my grandfather who was all I had in the way of a family and, to my taste, all that anyone could ask.

The shriveled leaves of the oak tree just outside my bedroom window formed grotesque patterns that were only faintly visible in the predawn light. The drizzling mist confirmed that the coming dawn would celebrate another typical Indiana winter morning. From trees drenched with moisture and eaves heavy with condensation, water would chime along the rainspouts to gather in ice-slivered puddles rimming the streets.

Prathersville, Indiana, under a sullen sky would plod its way towards another chill and early evening.

Sleep being gone, I snapped on my bedside lamp to look

4

for my book. Muttering a little, I fumbled for my fur slippers and a quilted robe. My grandfather's housekeeper is articulately explicit about the heavenly awards that accrue to people who practice thrift. Her campaign for a blessed after-life prompts her to embark on a relentless nightly pilgrim-age through the house to turn every thermostat to that precise point just above where the plumbing would freeze.

"That's all very well for you, Vinnie," I mumbled, bundling myself up. "You in your eiderdown snoring away like a cub curled for the winter, but it is hell for us night-walkers."

I knew exactly where I had left my book, beside the leather chair in the library downstairs. I slipped from my room silently and made my way along the polar wind tunnel that Vinnie calls the upper hall. In deepest darkness I could not lose myself in that house. For one thing, not a piece of furniture has been moved (except for cleaning) in the entire of my memory. And being the night person that I am, I had traveled those halls so many times that I could literally have done it blindfolded.

The nights of my childhood had not always been that secure. I had wakened to the frenzy of furious voices, to the finality of slammed doors in houses and apartments that served as way stations on the path that finally led my parents to divorce. But even then, like a small wary bat in a strange cave, I had learned that loneliness set on foot is at least a distraction.

As I padded along the hall towards the top of the stairs I noted that my grandfather's door was not latched. I paused and pushed it ajar to look in on him.

The door opened silently as I stepped into the room. I have watched my grandfather many times as he slept. There has always been an intriguing strangeness in his face in repose. With his eyes closed, their sadness is gone and the sense of hidden concern that lies behind them disappears. He is like an ivory memory of himself, untroubled.

To my astonishment, he was not asleep. I could see his silhouette upright against the pillows, his body spare against their roundness. He was staring silently at the predawn drizzle through his window as I had done only minutes before.

"Grand," I called softly, not to startle him. "Are you all right?"

He turned and stared at me, then spoke softly, not chuckling as I expected but with a tension in his voice that drew me nearer quickly.

"I must have summoned you with my thoughts, Chryseis," he said quietly. "Come and sit by me."

I pulled a low stool to his bedside and drew my robe closer.

"Now what is this nonsense about summoning me?" I asked lightly.

"I was thinking . . ." he caught himself midsentence and his voice trailed off. He tried to match my lightness of tone without much success. "What brings you padding about at this ungodly hour?"

"You of all people," I chided him. "Ungodly hour indeed. May I quote your own words. 'There are no Godless hours . . . somewhere above that mist Artemis rides! ' "

He caught my hand and held it tightly. "How well you are versed in my dead world, Chryseis. I hope you are equally well equipped for the live one you inhabit. I didn't waken you, did I?"

"With your dreaming silence?" I kidded. "Not likely. My eyes were open so I rose and walked. It was that simple."

"Restless Chryseis," he said thoughtfully. "No dream? No premonitions?"

"Of what should I be forewarned?" I asked brightly. "Did

the braised chicken liver of dinner betray some fateful augury . . . in among its mushrooms?"

To my surprise he did not respond to my kidding. His eyes slid from my face to the window behind me. In that dim light his flesh seemed almost translucent. The years that had stripped the padding from his face had exposed his high, well-shaped cheek bones and a slender aquiline nose that stood out in pale relief.

From the way his hand tightened on mine, I knew that what he was trying to say was urgently important to him. I waited silently, feeling a quickening of fear that I couldn't explain.

"You have read Plato," he said quietly. "You must remember his definition of a rich man . . . ?" his voice faded to a question.

"That the truly rich man is he who has made his proper offerings to the Gods and owes no man?" I asked.

He nodded, still not meeting my eyes.

"I have a debt, Chryseis," he said slowly and painfully. "I have a debt of such vital importance that having it unpaid bleeds the pleasure from my life. I have tried to pay it but I have been unable to—" His voice stopped on a note of surprise, as if he were newly astonished that he had been foiled in something so important to him.

"Can I help?" I asked, upset by his concern. "Can I do it for you?" But I was confused. I knew he was a man whose word was better than anyone else's bond and that certainly all his expenses were set promptly and cheerfully. What kind of a troubling debt could be this disturbing to his rest?

"The debt must be paid," he said slowly and carefully. "I have exhausted all avenues I know. But the debt must be paid, Chryseis, and I am at the end."

"Grand," I said firmly, "whatever this mysterious debt is,

7

I shall do it. I want to. I just need to understand. It will be done. I promise . . . but you must explain."

"There is a man," he said painfully, as if the revelation were drawn from his physical strength. "He is called Mathew Martin. I have lost him and he must be found."

"But there are ways, Grand," I assured him. "There are people who do nothing else but search for missing persons."

He shook his head vehemently. "It can't be done that way." His voice suddenly seemed harsh. "This must be a secret search and a secret finding."

His obvious agitation disturbed me. "Of course I'll help," I assured him. "We'll find him wherever he is."

"I did pretty well for a while," his voice was almost querulous. "I was able to find out when he enlisted for the service. Four years in Vietnam." There was a kind of pride in his voice as he said it. "But I couldn't reach him there and I waited." He paused and sighed. "Then after he was discharged I lost him," he paused again. "It shouldn't be too hard, should it, Chryseis? A veteran like that? The last report I got from the West Coast, but I was too ill to track him down."

"Was this a long time ago?" I asked. ". . . That he was discharged, I mean."

He shook his head. "Early this year. But they were only reports, you see, some contacts I had . . . just by chance. The thing is, Chryseis, that the debt must not be made public. Somehow, without publicity, or police, or any scandal, *he must be found.*"

"Trust me," I said carefully. "I will find Mathew Martin, and you will pay your debt to him—and secretly."

As we talked the sky had lightened beyond the window. A faint breeze stirred in the wilted leaves of the oak tree. My grandfather's face, in that ghostly light, was terrible to look at.

8

Only then did it occur to me that this strange debt to Mathew Martin could be a key to the sadness that had lain behind my grandfather's eyes ever since I could remember.

There was something more he wanted to say, but distressed by his excess of emotion, he only shook his head helplessly at me, gripping my hand tightly.

"We will find Mathew Martin," I repeated softly. "We will find him secretly as you wish . . . we'll start tomorrow."

He nodded and his head fell back tiredly, but his eyes still held mine. "Tomorrow I will tell you more," he said, and his voice trailed off.

I smiled at him as his eyes fluttered shut in an exhausted sleep. I watched him sleep, afraid to stir lest moving my hand away would waken him.

I sat there a long time in the growing dawn. I watched as light gradually illumined the room, the shelf of his favorite books, the triangle of oval portraits on the opposing wall. "His women" he called them—my grandmother, Margaret, my dead mother, Sylvia, and me, Chryseis, caught at sixteen in a half-frightened wide-eyed pose that I could never recognize as myself.

Suddenly the room was wholly lit. I could even see the smallest details of my grandfather's favorite painting that he had ordered moved up from the library as he spent more and more hours resting in his bed. The undecipherable name of its Italian painter sprawled across a corner whose frame was chipped from where I had hit it racing through the hall. It remained the favorite of all his collection.

With his hand still clasping mine I studied the picture for what must have been the millionth time. The narrow wooded lane passing through the darkness of giant trees; the man, tunic clad, lying beaten and at the point of death while his assailants stood a little aside dividing the spoils of their brutal robbery. Even on the flatness of canvas, the man's

9

dying lips always seemed to be moving as he raised a weak arm skyward to where a flock of cranes, brilliant in their grace, passed above the lowering trees.

I always hear the dying man's words spoken in the resonant tones of my grandfather's voice when he first explained the picture to me many years ago.

"Avenge me, O Cranes. Avenge Ibycus."

"But what happened?" I had asked, shocked at the violence of the scene.

"He was on the road to Corinth, as I have told you," my grandfather had explained quietly. "His friends waited and feared and waited more. He was journeying to the great celebration in the amphitheatre . . . thousands of people were gathering, and he, a famed poet, was to be among them.

"Finally they sent out servants to search for him. When they found him in the forest he was past all help.

"With heavy hearts, the friends of Ibycus joined the multitude and took their places on the benches that circled the huge theatre. First came the processional of the Fates . . . always the Fates in their terrible garb with masks of such horror that the immense crowd stilled with wonder and guilt and terror of the unknown.

"That day, even as the crowd grew silent, each man communing with his private terrors, a flock of white cranes, their feathers glistening in the sun of Corinth, flew overhead.

"They did not fly on. They circled and came lower and lower over the terrified multitude. As they circled ever lower, a man, frantic with terror, leaped to his feet and cried out, *'There they are . . . the cranes of Ibycus!'*

"A murmur passed through the crowd that had heard of the tragic death of a great poet. The man was seized with his companions. They readily admitted their guilt and were put to death."

My heart had thumped wildly as it always did with Grandfather's tales. "But what did it mean?" I asked. "Why did the cranes come?"

He had shrugged and laid an arm about my shoulder. "Nowadays when they mention the cranes of Ibycus, they mean 'Murder will out.' But the Greeks said it differently. They believed, as I do, that when all human means of justice have been exhausted, the Gods themselves will see that justice prevails."

"Do you believe that really?" I had asked. "Even now that all the Gods are gone?"

He had cupped his hand under my chin and smiled into my face. "Chryseis," he chided, half jesting, half soberly. "The Gods are not gone . . . only their names are changed."

"To protect the innocent?" I asked, pleased with my joke.

His laugh was rueful. "To protect the ignorant," he corrected me.

As Grand stirred in his sleep, his hand fell from mine. I made my way thoughtfully back down the hall to my own bed.

I did not go back to sleep for a long time. Strangely, I did not even dwell on who Mathew Martin was . . . Grand would explain in the morning. I just lay staring at the moving leaves beyond the window thinking how little I really knew of this man I loved so much.

Oh, I knew the bare facts of his life, and I certainly knew the facade that he presented to the world and to me. But under that lean, controlled exterior there must be another Jackson Lane Maxwell that I didn't really comprehend at all.

What strange compulsion had made him a lifelong Greek scholar even while he lived the humdrum life of a small-town banker? How had he been able, with such outward calm, to accept the loss of his loved ones . . . first his wife, then his beloved daughter Sylvia? How had he really felt

11

when he had been left, well into his later life, with a gawky, terrified twelve-year-old to raise?

And funny things. I knew he loved me and was loathe to deny me even my smallest desires. He obviously enjoyed my company or would not have planned the many trips we made together. Yet why had he so stubbornly (even truculently) refused to let me stay with him to live instead of packing me off to boarding school year after year so far away from him?

He must have had secret dreams that he abandoned for me. And from what mysterious secret passage of his life had come this Mathew Martin . . . this man with the run-of-the-phone-book name that he was so ominously indebted to?

I finally drifted off into a light sleep only to be wakened with shock at the abrupt sound of my door opening with such force that it banged against the wall. I leaped upwards clutching the covers.

Vinnie stood in the doorway of my room. Her left hand was still pressed against the open door. Her broad face was slack with shock, and with her free hand she made small vertical movements as if she were trying to lift her voice from the heaving cavern of her chest. Her lips moved soundlessly for a second before she emitted a shrill keening wail.

"He's gone," she wailed. "Dead in his sleep. Oh my God. Dead." Then she turned and fled down the hall as if pursued by demons.

I bent my head into my hands. The search for Mathew Martin was forgotten in the wave of tears that swept over me.

2

PRATHERSVILLE,
INDIANA

When my grandfather and I took our frequent holidays in Greece, we mostly spent our times in small villages that clung to ancient mountainsides with crumbling stubbornness. From such a village we started off one afternoon to pass the time until our host would have our evening meal prepared. We walked steadily upwards towards the blaze of bright sky, seeking to reach the highest point of all.

Being younger and brisker of leg, I ran around and ahead of Grand like a pup, exploring behind trees, looking for caves in the outcropping of rocks, searching for colored stones.

I went over a knoll that shut him from my view as he labored along on his pointed stick. Against the blue above me great birds wheeled and circled, their shadows changing the colors of the grasses.

Suddenly I realized that I was not alone. In the shadow of a wind-twisted tree I saw an old sheep bending over something in the long grass. It was nuzzling something gently, pushing and prodding. As I approached, the ewe raised its eyes to me. Her wool was straggled and soiled and thorny seeds were matted in its strands. I stared at her eyes, startled as I still always am at the sideways slit of the pupils. Only then, as I looked down, did I realize that the crumpled silent thing in the grass was her lamb.

I was staring at them, repulsed and hurting inside and at the point of tears, when my grandfather reached my side.

I gripped his hand tightly as he stood by me a moment in silence.

The dazed ewe ignored us. She had forgotten our presence as if we had been the wind that passed across the hill. She nudged at her dead lamb, poking it with a dumb stubbornness.

"What is she doing?" I whispered. "Why does she act like that?"

"She wants it to rise and walk," Grand said gently. "She does not know where its life has gone."

He led me away firmly. I remember my tears of helplessness as I looked back, with the great dark birds still circling overhead and the wind steady against our faces.

That scene came back to me again and again in the days that followed Grand's death. Everything that had to be done was so important, but between those acts lay hours of strange time that were disjointed and different somehow from the ordinary time of my life.

I found myself walking through the rooms of that house, not on any errand, just walking . . . touching things, the

14

sculpture, the lines of books, the urns that held the burgeoning houseplants. I was like something dumb and primitive nudging at the body of my grandfather's house, as if to stir it would bring back his lost life.

There was not a corner of that house that did not bring back his personality and his life . . . his simple and undramatic life that was woven inextricably with my own.

For although Grand had been born in the bed he died in, he was surely a man born out of his time. His father, the first Jackson Lane Maxwell, had not only built the house we lived in but also established the first bank in Prathersville. He had donated its only park, christened its hospital, and in some very subtle ways had set the pattern of the town so distinctively that even in the twentieth century the town still held the faint nineteenth century flavor of his personality.

So my grandfather was born to a role, if not a destiny. And he was a man poorly suited for the course life had set for him. He was docile enough, having gone to military school and then off to Harvard Business College, graduating with honors in the field his father chose for him.

But always inside he nurtured this private passion for the civilization of early Greece. He studied her poets, he knew the work of each sculptor, he must have literally memorized the face of ancient Greece by the time he was finally permitted to travel there for a two year "sabbatical" after finishing college. How he ever persuaded his father to give him that trip even he could not understand. It had been his father's despair that ever since he was old enough to trail a stubby finger across a page he had been absorbed by what the old man called "lost causes . . . lost times."

During those two idyllic years he wandered among ruins and museums and walked fabled islands and fell in love again . . . this time with a girl named Margaret Frazier, whose father was attached to our consular staff in Athens.

They might have stayed there forever except that the role was stronger than the dream. In 1923, the two of them returned to Prathersville, where Grand, his pale blue eyes still set on distant seas, grew into the job of president of his father's bank.

Under Grand's hand the old house that his father had built became an anachronism. There was not a room that did not bear the full flavor of his love for Greece. The room colors changed to the white of marble and alabaster or the luminous blues and greens of the Aegean Sea and sky. Marble statues, bas-reliefs, and treasures of cast bronze enriched every room. The wide stairway that rose from the foliage-filled lower hallway held a staggered collection of the etchings of Piranesi-like frozen memories rising towards sleep.

From the outside the house was totally different. It stood on its carefully groomed acre like the final castle of a fallen king. To the very sapling roots of his lilac hedge came the lawns of the invaders, small rectangles of besieged crabgrass indifferently adorned with young trees and containing in their carefully measured centers the shoebox houses of the postwar building boom.

But behind my grandfather's hedges, gnarled with age and humming with bees in their season, his house held back time with the relentless order of a banker's mind. The deep porches had gleaming ship-steel–colored wooden floors so smooth that I used to play jacks for hours with never a splinter from their polished surface.

The house itself was painted a deep Quaker gray with the trimming in white and a massive white door bearing the small brass knocker engraved with the simple legend, "Mr. and Mrs. Jackson Lane Maxwell".

Probably in truth that house had its weaknesses like all things built by man—roof repairs needed from time to time, a little shoring of the basement beams, and certainly a crack here and there that had to be spackled against the new wallpaper—but to me it was a great gray steady rock that my life leaned against.

So I moved numbly through the place that had always been my one place of comfort, the place I was sent back to when the uneasy climate of my parents' marriage erupted into storm.

I can't remember the first time I ever came, nor how many times there were. Sometimes I was very young, young enough to sway for hours on end in the swing beneath the big black walnut tree in the back yard, wearing the grass to hard clay with the toes of my sandals. Young enough to watch breathlessly when Vinnie was baking. She made what she called a "try" cake. It was a small cupcake that was baked before the final batter was committed to the oven. When the little cake was done she opened it with apprehension, studied its texture, and sniffed its fragrance before it was handed to me to devour. Then Vinnie, with her swift and efficient spatula, would divide the glossy batter into pans. Finally she would turn with a wry smile and scoop a generous dollop of the batter back into the bowl for me to eat on the back steps with leisurely ecstasy.

That strange, distracted week was broken by events. There was a long vigil at the funeral home where people came and went silently, as if in fear of wakening Grand—people I didn't know, whose names had never crossed my hearing. They said things to me that didn't matter at all, for they were not sentiments at all, only small reachings-out to this unknown girl of nineteen who was the only living remnant left of Jackson Maxwell.

I marveled at how little I knew of the life of the town and of my grandfather's friends. For even though Prathersville had been all the home I had ever been able to claim inside my heart, it was as if my grandfather had subtly kept me from it—and it from me. I had wanted too much to stay with him and Vinnie and go to public school with the children of the town. My grandfather would not hear of it. When summer came and I was free, I wanted nothing so much as to spend the lazy warmth of that season in this sleepy town, but always there was a trip planned, or later, when he ceased to travel, a special experience for me—always away.

Now he was gone and those few selected people that Grand had let me know could almost be numbered on my fingers. There was Mr. McAllister, who had replaced my grandfather at the bank, and his quiet dark-eyed wife Ellie. Miss Emily Lord I knew. She had taught Latin in Prathersville since her youth and lived in sombre gentility in the old family house on Court Street. There were several relatives of Melanie's, my only friend, but they were only faceless cousins who came bearing sympathy, not people whose eyes I could meet with any understanding.

They came and talked a while and left, their faces drawn into the proper attitudes of grief, and Vinnie let them out as she had let them in, without anything's changing.

I looked at the names on the great floral displays and on the single wreath of laurel leaves that came from Melanie's Aunt Tru and thought about Mel and how much I wished she were not so far away. Even after what the years had done to our friendship, she still stood alone as the only "best friend" I ever had in my life.

The Lyons, like the Maxwells, were "old families" in Prathersville. They ran the grain mill and elevator for the agricultural area that stretched away from the little town. Melanie Lyons was older than I, by about five years, but we were thrown together in that social way that small-town children are. She went to school in Prathersville and lived there all her life. I came and went like a swallow and was always in private school, so our friendship was an interrupted thing—lacking the tedium of overexposure that might have robbed it of flavor.

At first I remember our staring at each other with the natural hostility of forced friendship while our families dined or spent afternoons together—her mother pale and elegant, her outrageous Aunt Tru (whom I feared and adored), and her father, bluff and red-faced and genial.

When we finally did get to be friends, it was fabulous. Off at private school I would be lonely and think about Mel and how it would be to tell her of things. For Mel is a secret person.

Once removed from the vigilance of her overbearing mother, Melanie became a fey wisp of a person whose magnetic eyes concealed plans of daring and something almost magical. Her wit was quick and her disposition sunny, but always behind it lay a strange unexpected quirk of the unpredictable.

It was Mel who introduced me to terrifying rites of witchcraft, which she had carefully cribbed from library books that she dared not check out and take home. One year we tried potions and spells and alchemy. The potions were dreadful and the spells didn't work and nothing ever changed to gold, but some accidental success with predictions that we wrote and solemnly buried under the bricks in our playhouse scared us both a little.

I must have been seven and she about twelve the year we took over the summer house not as an ornament but as a play house, and then a club (very exclusive—no boys). Not that any boys would have cared to invade that sanctuary of ragged dolls and broken tea sets!

Our friendship that wove in and out of the years survived time but not circumstance. The year I was twelve going on thirteen, my mother married again. I was dressed like a doll for the occasion and watched with a numbed confusion as my mother, glowing with her incredible beauty, moved among the guests on the arm of this Arthur Hall whom I barely knew but was supposed to be "Father."

I can still evoke the scent of my mother's perfume as she bent to kiss me good-bye.

"When we get back, Chryseis," she said softly, her eyes gleaming, "we will have such fun together . . . all of us." She had glanced up at her new husband. "We will have parties and fun picnics and all the things you like. Just be good and remember, Mother loves you."

Mostly I remembered the loneliness of her being away and not getting to go back to Grand's like I used to. I had to go back and forth to school with a strange housekeeper at home. She was a dour woman whose name I never got right so that she was always correcting me crossly.

Then there was the telegram. Then the tears. Then the final nightmare acceptance that my mother and her new husband had indeed been on the plane that went down in the Circassian Mountains, and it was all over.

That was when I came back to Grand's house for real and forever . . . I thought.

But in a way Mel had gone away as thoroughly as my mother had. The summer that had brought tragedy to me had struck the same kind of blow to Melanie.

Mel's father ran the Prathersville Mill, which had been a landmark since settlement days. I had always heard it referred to as a "firetrap," with its aging timbers dried with time and thickened with the crusty chaff of a legion of harvests. But firetrap or not, an institution it was, the noisy steaming nucleus of the community, with trucks coming and going with loads of feed or fertilizer, tractors and combines straddling their pools of oil in the littered yards, and always the huddles of farmers and their sons gathered in gossip about weather and crops or somebody's great stud bull.

It was probably inevitable that someday that combination of volatile circumstances would trigger tragedy. It could have been anything—a carelessly tossed match, a magnified stray of sunlight through a pane of glass. How the fire began no one ever knew. The holocaust came. The mill blazed skyward in early evening when the normal complement of employees who might have been there to battle the blaze were off to supper or the evening. The torch of its burning illumined the prairie sky for miles around, and there were tales of farmers miles away whose lawns were blackened by airborne cinders.

It was late the following day before the blaze was finally under complete control, and the volunteer firemen, threading their way through the blackened smoking ruins, found the charred shell of what had once been the warm bluff soul of Ambrose Lyons. Everyone knew his habits of lingering late over his books in the upper office. No one was surprised that he had been trapped by smoke or fumes and been unable to escape the hell his world had turned to.

But Mel was never the same to me after that. She was a strange walking shadow of herself, older than her years or my memory. We stood apart from each other in the mutual separateness of our griefs and, embarrassed by them, stayed apart.

She was married a year later, to an older man whom I never met, a man who had managed the mill for her father. If I was even invited to the wedding I was not told of it. The news of her marriage came to me almost indirectly. Grand, who wrote regularly, never mentioned it. Vinnie, who wrote only occasionally, sent me a clipping from the paper. The write-up was very burbling, the way they are in small town papers when a local belle is married. There were long

21

descriptions of the attendants and the gowns and the music of the ceremony. It also stated that the young couple were moving to the San Francisco area after a brief sojourn abroad. It all sounded so stuffy and so unlike Mel that I stared at the picture in disbelief.

She was beautiful as always but unsmiling in a pillar of white lace with a trailing train. She held trailing ribbons and sprays of stephanotis between herself and the camera lens like a shield.

So Mel had faded into the new identity of Mrs. Brandon North in a place I had never seen, leaving me with only summer memories and a vague longing for an intimacy that was beyond recall.

The house stayed full of people clear through the day of the funeral. But they drifted away with the light of that day, leaving the great empty rooms of the house emptied of all but Vinnie and me for the first time in days.

I undressed with a sense of release. I loosened my hair and brushed it hard as if to ease the weight of the days past with the rigors of movement. I stared at myself in the mirror thinking about tomorrow . . . not *really* tomorrow, but just the day that would come after this day and the things I had to do.

I must tear myself away from the protection of these walls and begin an ordinary life again. I would have to drive the car, to go to the bank that I knew so well and have a conference with Mr. McAllister about the details of the trust that Grand had set up for me.

I knew in essence what that trust would be. Grand had talked of it to me many times. I would be on an allowance to cover my schooling and other expenses until I was twenty-five. At that time I would inherit this house, these grounds, and that undisclosed amount of property that comprised his estate. I would inherit my grandfather's world as I had inherited his height, his blue eyes, and his love of ancient Greek lyric poets.

I was hanging my head down like a child, feeling that marvelous prickly feeling of a scalp relieved of its burden of imprisoned hair. I was startled to hear Vinnie's rapid, heavy tread on the stairs. My head was still upside down when she burst into my room.

"Get some clothes on," she ordered resentfully. "You got another caller coming. It's Miss Tru Lyons. I saw her paying a cab out front."

I threw my hair back and stared at her.

"But she's in California," I protested, "with Melanie. She had the laurel wreath sent—the one I put into Grand's coffin."

"Not now she isn't," Vinnie said crossly. "I just thought you might like a warning."

She disappeared to answer the pealing of the bell already sounding downstairs.

3

THE SMALLER WORLD OF
JACKSON MAXWELL

The reality of time is so vulnerable to sounds remembered.
How many times the keening of a fog horn has reduced me to
the shivering child I was when Mother and I shared an apart-
ment near the East River many years ago! The barest melodic
bones of a certain song my mother used to hum can make me
the gawky colt of the summer before she died! The brusque
sounds of Miss Tru's voice in the hall below stopped my
brush and brought back a flood of memories of school
holidays with the fireplace heaped with greens and snow-
flakes etched against clouded windows as guests moved
through the festive rooms.

Feeling more child than woman, I threw on a caftan and
wound my hair around my head to go and join her and
Vinnie in the hall below.

Tru Lyons, or Miss Tru, as I always thought of her, was old to me even in my childhood. She was always just there—with her outrageous opinions stilling the conversation in drawing rooms, her uneven elegance, the badly fitted dress of excellent color and design worn with shoes overrun at the heel and stockings whose seams scurried sideways up her thin legs.

In a town like Prathersville everyone does something. The roles are stamped on people so tightly that it always seemed that to fall from one's slot would be to fall endlessly, down and down and out of the real world of chatter and commerce and child raising into some limbo of nonbeing.

Miss Tru was unique in that she had no real role in the town.

From a far perspective she might seem to be an average aging spinster of independent means whose roses bloomed extravagantly in their monthly cycles and who inspired her petunias to produce fragrance that strayed across the hedges to flavor a whole block.

She was about as average as a unicorn.

In Prathersville it was de rigueur for spinsters of Miss Tru's vintage to support with their checkbooks and their sturdy legs the local institutions: the church, the women's club, and various other afternoon organizations that kept penury from the young, the old, and those merchants clever enough to stock conservatively designed jersey dresses in half sizes.

Miss Tru "belonged" only to the human race, and that because she had been enlisted at an age too young for protest. She loathed women "in concert," as she called them, and considered all philanthropy self-conscious meddling. She had publicly denounced the First Presbyterian Church of Prathersville as an architectural monstrosity and its minister by more earthy and less acceptable epithets.

Miss Tru did nothing. Being thus without a role in the

larger drama of the town's life, words fell from people's lips hastily in an attempt to define her function.

"Ambrose's sister is an artist," I once heard Mel's mother explain. An irritated grimace crossed Miss Tru's face.

"Oh, you paint?" the delighted question came.

"Only barns," Miss Tru muttered truculently, turning away.

"But what does she really do . . . with her time, I mean?" I asked Mel, who adored her.

Mel's eyes brightened and her breath quickened a little. "Whatever she wants to," she said in an almost conspiratorial tone. "All the time, whatever she wants to, can you imagine?"

I shook my head. I couldn't imagine that. "And she never gets bored?"

Mel shook her head, smiling secretly. "Not her. She has books all over that Mother won't even let me look at the covers of, and she gardens when she wants, and sometimes she doesn't get up at all."

"Not all day?"

Mel giggled. "When Auntie does that, Mother pulls her mouth down tight and says she is 'indisposed'—but she isn't. She just lets the world make it without her—'keeping it honest,' she calls it."

"But the painting?"

"Oh, she paints too, but she also knits and cooks and makes rose-hip jam and keeps a journal—writes in it every day of her life. She walks a lot, at night by herself. She's great . . . and lucky," Mel added wistfully.

"But she's an old maid," I pointed out. "Isn't she lonely?"

"Not her," Mel said. "She has too many people who just like her—not only family, but funny people who come and sit and talk with her in the garden and by her fire on winter evenings. I know people giggle about her being a character,

26

the way she walks at night with the shepherd's crook kind of cane she has and all, but I don't care."

"And she isn't afraid ever?" I wondered.

Mel laughed. "She always says she would only be afraid of the devil if he appeared as a boxer with his teeth bared."

But that was a long time ago. Miss Tru's big house on Court Street had been a boarding house for transients for years. The petunias were gone from beside the walk, and few roses bloomed on the bushes that were trimmed for tidiness, not growth. She had been off in California living near Mel for a long time. Yet here she was, following her laurel wreath with her own hoarse voice, admonishing Vinnie in the lower hall.

I descended the stair quietly. I needn't have. The flurry of activity she had raised about her just by the power of her personality would have drowned out even a stamping descent.

She was wearing a fine English tweed of some muted olive with sienna accents. It sagged with the pressure of hours of sitting since its last trip to the cleaners. She was struggling out of galoshes while Vinnie helplessly watched.

Age had only diminished her. She was shorter, sparer, and larger of nose than I remembered, but the essence was the same, the quick rush of brusque tones and the rapid movements that made the hall fairly vibrate with her excess of vitality.

"Couldn't stand to come at the proper time," she was explaining. "All those people mewling in here with over-baked ham and half-baked sentiments. Thought I'd come by late and catch you alone." She gave a quick piercing glance at Vinnie. "You do have macaroni salad and angel cakes out of your mind, don't you?"

Vinnie nodded helplessly.

"Mostly I want to see Chryseis, and it seemed the best time."

When she noticed me coming down the stairs, she stared at me a moment silently, then shook her head. "How like your mother you are and yet so different." She knelt to her galosh again, still talking. "Every bit as beautiful, but with the look of having your head screwed on, which she certainly never did. Taller too, but then that's the way they're doing it these days. They'd have put a brick on you a generation ago to hold you down."

Her flow of words suddenly stopped and she smiled at me, a half-cocked grin that gave her face a rakish air.

"But there you are . . . Chryseis," then she added more softly, "The Gods came through for him, didn't they? Having you here with him when the end came. But the Gods always loved him," she added quietly.

When she pressed her lips to my cheeks, her skin was moist and cold from the evening. She smelled of potpourri and the out-of-doors all at once.

"And you, child?"

I nodded. "I'm fine," I told her. "It's Vinnie who's been worn ragged."

"Nonsense," she said shortly, looking squarely at Vinnie. "There's never been a life or a death that could phase *her*. She's the pillar, the tower . . . I could go on. But she will need a rest after this, a long stay away from here . . . somewhere warm . . ." She was eyeing Vinnie so speculatively that Vinnie spoke quickly.

"Just what we've planned, thank you, Miss Tru," she said quickly to forestall an avalanche of suggestions. "I'm taking off for a while . . . to rest, as you say."

"Good. Good," Miss Tru nodded her head smartly.

"Now you," she turned back to me purposefully.

I steered her towards the library where she perched nervously on the edge of a chair. "You can't imagine how

28

glad I am you came," I told her. "Really, do stay for supper with me . . . all cold from the fridge with no fuss."

She studied my face a minute then nodded sharply, "I'd really like that."

"Then find a better chair while I speak to Vinnie."

"That's uppity enough," Vinnie was grumbling in the kitchen. "Inviting herself for dinner to a house of sorrow."

"She doesn't mean it that way," I protested, setting the teakettle to boil. "She knew we would have a let-down . . . and she's lonely too. Where do you suppose she's staying?"

"Not in her own house surely," Vinnie paused with a stricken look. "Not the way that Mrs. Jensen runs it, smelling of Lysol and old dirt."

"Cold ham and some of those rolls from a tin heated and all the salads," I suggested, setting things out. "It wouldn't put you out for her to stay here would it? In case I asked?"

Vinnie stared at me a minute and then frowned for a transient moment. I thought she might cry. She ducked her head and breathed hard and then said gruffly, "You're *him* again, Chrys. Anyway, it's your house."

I laid my hand a minute on her arm and started back to my guest.

Miss Tru had left the stiff chair as I suggested and was standing in the middle of the room. Her eyes moved slowly about it, as if she were visually stroking the deep bookcases that lined the wall, the small sculpture with the absent nose, the stack of pipes, and the pile of current and unread periodicals that heavied the drum table by the leather chair.

I waited. Something was happening in the room that I didn't really understand. The essence of my grandfather seemed to grow stronger. I could suddenly smell the pungency of his pipe smoke still caught in the drapes, his chuckle sounding in the dying embers of the hearth fire.

29

When she turned to me, a slow unheeded trickle of moisture moved down the lines of her cheeks.

"I came here to be with him for the last time," she explained simply. "I have loved him, with varying densities, since we were children here together in this Godforsaken place. But he peopled it with Gods, Jackson did, his own Gods, wrested from a bunch of rotting books.

"What hours we spent you couldn't believe, Chryseis, although you were always a secret person too, you and Mel. But Jackson grew up and away and found your grandmother." She shrugged.

She sank into Grand's great leather chair, her sparrowy fingers spread like bird claws across the fullness of its arms. She stared into the fire thoughtfully.

"After the pain of that was gone, we got to be friends again. Jackson's Margaret died leaving him with your mother to raise—with problems and all. When she was away—"

"Away? My mother?" I interrupted, intrigued. "I thought she grew up here—like Mel."

Miss Tru barely noticed the interruption. "When she went east to school that year . . . her last year of high school I guess it was . . . after that it was never the same. She got married, and then it was one thing and another, trouble with your father, and finally the divorce."

"But I never realized Mother went away at all," I remarked again. "Why did she do that?"

Miss Tru shook her head. "Who understands girls? Why did I grow up to be such a truculent old tart? Why did Mel turn so strange and withdrawn when she grew up? For that matter, why are you, a big lovely nineteen-year-old sitting around wasting time with an old baggage like me?"

"Because I want you here," I giggled, meaning it.

She grinned, but her expression changed quickly. "So the years went away, and Jackson was always too busy to need

30

me. I would have married him if he had asked me." She laughed almost merrily. "He came close a couple of times; when Sylvia was very young. But he never did get around to it. I have never told this to a soul, living or dead, Chryseis. I would have married your grandfather any minute of his life, but it got too late too soon. He didn't need me. Never knew you were third in a triangle, did you, child?"

I shook my head helplessly.

"A woman," she said slowly, "even an old, shriveled haggard woman like myself, can only put her love where it is needed, Chrys. That's why I finally went away, and that's why I'm back here now."

"I don't understand," I said helplessly.

"Everyone who knew Jackson liked him, Chryseis," she said slowly. "But few of us were privileged to love him. That's what you and I have in common. We are the last living souls in the world who knew, understood, and loved Jackson Maxwell. I wanted to tell you that you are not a homeless orphan at all. Wherever Jackson Maxwell is loved is your home. You'll go back to school and summer will come. If something gay and hip and mod comes up that you want to do, take off. But when you are lonely or lost or between things, please come home, Chrys. Come home to me."

It was a plea, gently stated but roughly spoken, almost a command. I went to her quickly and caught her lean spareness in my arms. I guess we clung there wordlessly just long enough for me to understand what I had failed to grasp. This was what I needed, someone else who shared that one thing—a love for Grand.

Then, characteristically, she pushed me away almost roughly.

"Miserable thing, flying. Never fly when you can drive, never drive when you can walk, and never walk where there isn't a leash law. You'll like walking where I live. It's always half heaven and half hell. It's so hilly that your only choice is to go panting among hills, going or coming. But there are still deer among the trees and the smell of chaparral plants in the air.

"Terrible house. But I always keep a terrible house. People spend their lives putting things away that they need to get right out again. I never do that." She spread her hands wide, "Books and aborted paintings and masses of white daisies everywhere, and your room overlooks the bay. Any time. All the time, if you want.

"I do hope that's potato salad as well as macaroni. For some reason the pepper turns rank in macaroni salad quicker."

I giggled and went to see how Vinnie was doing with dinner.

There was lean sliced ham with a crisp, sugary edge surprising the first bite, both macaroni and potato salad, and a marvelous one of mixed kinds of beans splendid with pimiento. We ate lustily for a long time. Mostly Miss Tru talked as I listened, but something settled into me with a gentle content. A place I didn't know I had opened like a hidden door in a dark wall. A home I had never seen, which clung (precariously, she said) to the hills of Sausalito, was suddenly inviting me.

Because I led her on, she talked a lot about Mel and the man she married.

"There wouldn't have been any reason for you to know the North family," she dismissed them curtly. "People without any style at all, except for Brandon himself. And he's so much older that even if you had come across him, you'd have never remembered."

"But Mel married him," I protested. "She's not that much older than I."

"True, true," she nodded thoughtfully. "Well, they were thrown together from the beginning. Brandon was helping my brother manage the mill. Why Bran has as much as admitted that he has been in love with that child since she was a tot. He sent her flowers on her first teen birthday I remember, did all kinds of romantic, gallant things like that."

"You'd think her family would object, an older man paying court to her like that."

"Bran's a different kind of man," Miss Tru said thoughtfully. "Doesn't look his age . . . not in any way. And he's got that light charm, sophistication . . . education . . . everything."

"A miller?" I asked, not meaning to sound caustic. But the picture she was drawing was ever so much more cosmopolitan than the man I associated with a mill in a country town.

"Oh, that," she said lightly. "That makes him sound different from what he is. He was in the war of course, a great hobby man, has a gun collection that is insured for some unbelievable amount . . . they scare Mel to death, incidentally, that great wall of locked walnut cabinets with guns from every country, every century. Other than that obsession with firearms, he is a kind of scientist. He went to school under the G.I. Bill and came out an agronomist. A good one too, I wager, because he is successful out of your mind. It was right after he and Mel returned from their honeymoon abroad that he joined this import-export firm in California." She paused and stared at me. "I guess I never thought about it, but that's probably why he ever came back to Prathersville at all . . . to wait for Mel. He's idolized her all her life and is the most adoring husband that ever turned your stomach. It's unrealistic!" She shrugged. "Men."

"But they really never got together until after the fire?" I asked.

She stared at me again that funny way, as if I had said something illuminating. "That's right. And I remember that it surprised me. She was so depressed after her father died. For some reason it was Brandon she turned to, and a barely decent year later they got married."

"Happy ever after?" I asked lightly.

"He adores her. They have a magnificent house, lots of friends—mostly his, I think," she shook her head. "She's always been different since then. I can't figure her out. A strange, fey girl."

I tried to coax her to stay the night but she would have none of it. "Remember the old Japanese fellow who had the great truck garden out east of town?" she asked irrelevantly.

I shook my head. She rose, making a cursory gesture towards smoothing her rumpled skirt. "Sold fresh vegetables on the corner by the bank for years," she explained. "Great old gentleman. Corby tells me he's laid up, and has been for a year. I plan to pop out there in the morning for a chat and then catch an early afternoon plane home. God, how I hate flying."

I thought of Mel's phrase—"Auntie's funny friends."

"You'll come," she said with finality when I helped her wrap for the cab she called.

"I'll come," I promised and kissed her lightly.

She chattered on as we walked down the long walk to where the cab would stop in the street. As I watched the cab lights retreat down the deserted wet street, I felt curiously different.

The rain had stopped, but the fog was heavy like spun sugar in the night air. Everything looked unreal and altered; the lilac bushes stood in the mist like shrouded giants guarding me and the house they hid from the world.

The fog had thickened so that the world was narrowed to the confines of the yard, and I shivered.

34

The night was a metaphor for Grand's life.

In those early years, the green lawn had stretched out for twelve acres around the house itself. Carefully tended paths had led to the everywheres of my childhood. There had been the carriage house, vast and cavernous with memories of stale hay lingering in its shadowy depths, and the summer house that Melanie and I had shared, its windowless walls available to the hearts of the giant oaks where we could oversee, unnoticed, the domestic concerns of each generation of birds.

For the first time it occurred to me to wonder why Grand had sold all those acres off and let the ugly development enclose his small sanctuary. Had it been for money? It seemed unlikely.

Maybe it was a part of his withdrawal from life and its involvements.

I had watched him, one by one, give up many things. We stopped traveling. He gave up his positions in the community, turning the reins of the bank over to Mr. McAllister, even resigning his place on the board of trustees of the state university.

I shivered my way back up the long path. His world had shrunk to smaller gardens, then to the house itself as his health failed. In the end, in fact, his life was almost wholly led in that airy upper room with its great painting of the Cranes of Ibycus and a few favored books.

Would it have been different if he and Miss Tru had ever drawn together in their loneliness? As I locked the door and drew the bolt behind me, I pondered Miss Tru's appeal to me. The house was already beginning to feel of Grand's death more than his life. I knew that I would end up going to her, seeking out that strange woman in her untidy house in Sausalito as a sort of sentimental journey

. . . to get back in touch with Grand through the other living soul who loved him as I did.

That's what I thought then, but the search for Mathew Martin had been pressed from my mind. It was to return.

4

CORNERS WEST

A stuffed pheasant, its plumage ruffled fiercely, stared at me with unseeing eyes from the pedestal in Mr. McAllister's office. That same pedestal had held a statue of Praxiteles' Hermes when this office had been my grandfather's domain. But the walls had been white then, not the darkly knotted paneling that reduced the room to a sombre, dark enclosure.

Having patiently reiterated all the terms of the trust agreement that Grand had explained to me many times, Mr. McAllister made some small talk about my coming semester at college and then stood as a signal that our business was over.

I was already at the door when he suddenly remembered. "Ye Gods, Chrys," he said in an exasperated tone, totally unlike the "banker's" voice he had been using. "I almost forgot."

He reopened the file he had placed on his desk and pulled a small envelope from it. "This is for you. It is a separate safe deposit box—separate from the one your grandfather kept his legal documents in. He has kept it a long time but seldom entered it that I noticed. In any case, you are to have access to it. It was his request."

I took the long narrow key in my hand and looked at it.

"You might just want to look through it while you are here," he suggested. "Miss Verling will help you."

Back in a formal cubicle, I opened the box. I don't know what I expected . . . things of my mother's I guess . . . more papers maybe. The box was almost entirely filled by a large rectangular package wrapped in brown mailing paper and carefully sealed along each edge. A label had been neatly centered on its face. In my grandfather's clear Spencerian script was written, "Personal . . . for Mathew Martin."

I sat there a long time turning the sealed package in my hands, trying to recall my grandfather's precise words. "I have a debt of such vital importance that it bleeds the pleasure from my life," he had said. This mysterious package brought back Grand's request with all its terrible urgency.

I breathed deeply, replaced the package in the box and rang for Miss Verling.

Unlike my grandfather's office, Miss Verling hadn't changed. She might have been just a mite broader across the corset than in my youth, but her yellow marcelled hair with the pink skin gleaming through was unchanged, even to a small moist bun on her neck that prickled with an armament of copper-colored pins. She pressed the buzzer and let me out into the lobby of the bank.

"You'll be back at school now, I suppose, Chrys," she said companionably as she held open the small door.

"Probably," I nodded.

"The Spencer boy left only yesterday," she went on, "and Natalie . . ."

I must have stopped stock-still as it struck me.

"You must know every one in this town, Miss Verling," I said with undisguised interest.

"There was a time that I did," she said almost apologetically. "But things have changed so much, so many new businesses, and people coming and going the way they do." She looked vexed, as if some conspiracy of motility had robbed her of her special feel for the pulse of the town.

"It's that way everywhere, I'm sure," I said placatingly. "It's just that I miss the old friends I had . . . Melanie for instance."

She nodded sympathetically. "She's a real loss. Such a nice girl. But you can't blame her for wanting to get away from here after the fire and all. Such a miserable way for her father to die . . . burned to death in an accident like that. And they were always so close, coming in here hand in hand when she was no taller than his trouser pocket." She sighed. "But they all leave sooner or later . . . the young ones all leave."

"I wonder," I said as casually as possible. "Did you ever know a Mathew Martin?"

"Martin," she repeated thoughtfully. "The Martins over on Riverdale had only girls, Debra and Susan. There was a Martin family that had the Ford agency for a while right after the war." She frowned, probing her cerebral file under its thin layer of hair. "Then there's the Martin that runs the store out at Corners West. I seem to remember that he had a son called Mat . . ." Her voice trailed off in an irritated half question.

"It's not important," I assured her, hoping to get away

39

before she started a natural sequence of questions like, "How old a man is he?" and so forth.

As I eased the car out of the bank parking lot, I went over her small store of information. Debra and Susan were out, of course, and the Ford agency had been called Lansing ever since I could remember. On a moment's impulse, I circled the block and started out toward Corners West . . . just for kicks.

The west road out of Prathersville is no scenic route. It's really the wrong side of town for houses. What residences there are scatter irregularly along the highway in a sort of random fashion. The houses are small and ill-designed and seemingly held together only by layers of peeling paint.

There is a car dealer or so, a number of small franchise establishments where teen-agers flock on humming summer nights. Then, when everything seems to have stopped for lack of interest, you reach the Prathersville Mill.

The new mill is gleaming and shiny, with metal storage tanks and a great army of bright harvesting equipment offered for sale. Behind the mill are repair yards that inadvertently advertise the obsolescence of the product by being filled with crowded, dusty ancestors of the latest thing in harvesting or plowing.

I hate even driving by the new mill. I have never been in it. The old mill was something else . . . a great brick shell with cavernous rooms and a small untidy office on the second floor where Mel's father sweated among his books. The storage areas below were dim and secret and fragrant with the scent of hay and alfalfa. Mel and I loved to play hide-and-seek among the bales of bound hay, and hear, in our silences, the rustle of mice making their furtive escapes through the light that filtered dimly through high windows.

All that was gone after the fire, and the metal storage bins looked antiseptic and forbidding to me.

Beyond the mill lay only fields and cattle grazing in the snow-stained meadows, gathered in chilled huddled groups with their backs to the afternoon wind.

"Corners West," as Miss Verling called it, was really just a junction of a farm-to-market road with the state highway. An orange service station decorated one corner, and on the opposing side, a huge loading pen for cattle had been built along with the sturdy fenced corner of someone's land. The third building was a long wooden structure, which began at the front as a store and somehow seemed to end up as a house with curtains at the windows and a storage tank for butane gas only carelessly concealed by a latticework of fence. An aging pick-up truck stood at the back door. The faded wooden sign out front labeled the place simply enough as MARTIN'S STORE.

A bell rang somewhere in the back of the store as I entered. This was no supermarket, that was for sure. The walls of canned goods were dusty, and the counter by the cash register was stacked with displays, left, I presumed, by some optimistic salesman.

It did smell good. A mingled aroma of dill vinegar and the faint decaying scent of giant home-cured hams, which hung from high hooks along the wall behind the small meat counter, hit me as I went inside.

An older man in blue bib overalls appeared instantly from behind a loose cloth curtain, as if an instant's delay would tempt the customer to steal the very crackers from his barrel.

He was a big man whose hair went from white to gray down the sides of his head as if the color was draining from him by gravity even as his huge body sloped into the charity of his loose-cut overalls. I didn't like him right off. His face seemed to have congealed into lines of chronic anger or discontent.

41

"Help you?" he asked in a surly tone, as if I had interrupted him from great pleasure for no reason.

"Coke," I improvised swiftly. "Could I have a carton of Coke?"

Maybe it was my consciousness of my trumped-up errand that made his glance seem suspicious.

"Cold or nay?" he asked shortly.

"Cold," I replied, desperately trying to think of some way to thaw him from his monosyllables.

He watched my hands as I counted out the change, and I was angry that his scrutiny made me awkward and trembly.

"Oh, by the way," I tried to sound casual as he shook a bag open for my purchase, "do you happen to know a Mathew Martin around here?"

It couldn't be my imagination that time. His hands stilled, and his whole body stiffened at my words. A sudden wave of almost palpable hostility struck me as he raised his eyes to mine.

"That I do not," he said angrily. "No one of that name. No son of mine."

I shrugged and started for the door almost skittering. He came out from behind the counter and stood there, glaring at me challengingly.

"How come you ask?"

I paused, feeling a little more secure with my hand on the door knob. "I thought I remembered," I said helplessly, "a long time ago . . ."

"From school, I guess," his anger seemed to abate a little, and he rested a hand on the untidy counter. "No son of mine," he repeated. Then he turned his broad back to me and started towards the curtained door. The bell rang dismally as I made my escape, standing still a moment just outside the door to catch my breath.

I set the parcel on the floor and fished for my car keys.

As I turned the key in the ignition, my attention was caught by a movement at a window near the back of the house. Someone was watching me from behind that limp curtain. It couldn't be that cross old man. He hadn't had time to get back there that fast without running. I couldn't make out a face at all, for the features were obscured by the cloud of dirt on the window and the loop of curtain that swayed against it.

With a shiver of distaste I swung out onto the highway towards home.

I finished the errands that I had set myself with a sense of strange detachment. I could not seem to shake the apprehension that followed me away from Martin's Store. The day bled away towards early twilight by the time I made my last stop at Miss Emily Lord's house to deliver a lovely blue and white casserole that had come to the house filled with something fishy and scalloped that Vinnie and I had really enjoyed.

The Lord house was the same vintage as my grandfather's but more modest in scale. The house chattered to itself companionably as I stood on the porch waiting. The skeleton of a wisteria vine tapped some message to the porch pillar, and the wind forced a faint squeal of protest from the second-story shutters above my head.

This house that had once burst with children now housed only old Mrs. Lord and Miss Emily, who had remained a spinster and stayed on to teach Latin to less and less interested students at Prathersville High. I always liked Miss Emily, her straight-eyed look and the patrician stiffness of her carriage.

When she answered the door, she immediately pressed me with hospitality.

"Do come in and have tea," she urged, "or even a little sherry. I know you're too young, but I haven't done anything illegal all day. I'll miss your grandfather, you know," she tossed over her shoulder as she preceded me down the hall.

"I know," I agreed, shrugging out of my coat.

"The same wavelength," she commented quietly, "give or take a century!"

An overweight yellow cat stared at me with almond eyes from the windowsill as Miss Emily filled the teapot.

"Mother is resting up for dinner," she explained wryly. The cat rose, stretched, and leaped to the floor beside her, his tail curled imperiously. He looked up at her and yowled.

Obediently she bent to fill his dish.

"Our ménage à trois," she explained. "Two women and a male cat with a dominance psychosis . . . classic and comfortable."

We took our tea in the sitting room where Miss Emily worked. The conversation slid from topic to topic, the way it does between people who share nothing except basically good vibrations.

We talked about my grandfather, the changes in the town, and the crowd in the old days when I used to come home for holidays. I told her about Miss Tru's visit and her invitation.

"You ought to go," she said heartily. "Some day I'm going to break away myself. That's the one place in the country I've always wanted to visit . . . and of course Mel is there too."

"Mel is about the only young friend I ever had here," I admitted. Then on impulse, I said, "Do you remember a Mathew Martin?"

"Martin . . ." she repeated thoughtfully. "Common name, Mathew. Oh, I do remember . . . with one 't,' which was something to remember since I always considered it barbaric to change the spelling like that. A little older than you, wasn't he?" She tightened her lips, figuring. "Well, he was

44

to be a senior the year of the fire. That would make him . . . thirty anyway."

" 'Was to have been?' " I asked her. "Did he leave or something?"

"I guess so. I was disappointed . . . very good at language, one of the best I had. But he didn't come back his senior year. No idea why, but since that was not a family we knew, I never heard any more about him."

When I rose to leave for home, it was dead dark beyond the windows. I called Vinnie to let her know I was on my way.

"Be careful," Vinnie cautioned, "the road is wet. Some woman was here to see you but she left. Didn't leave her name. Soup all right?"

"Excellent," I assured her, grinning. I knew that to Vinnie "soup" meant beginning in the morning with a fat hen and bay leaves and homemade noodles patiently drying on a bread board.

As I backed Grand's car out Miss Emily's drive, I saw a light come on upstairs in the Lord house. Mrs. Lord was rising from rest to dine in order to sleep again. Nowhere but Prathersville, I thought.

Before I got to our driveway I noticed a pick-up truck parked at the house next door. As my headlights swept it, I glimpsed a figure sitting in the driver's seat, but the instant of light was so quick that I started my hassle with the garage door without thinking much about it.

Vinnie had turned on the porch light for me. The light flooded the wide porch with only a little spilling onto the dark stairs.

I had almost reached that patch of light with my arms loaded with bundles when a woman appeared suddenly, as if from among the shrubs.

"You're the Maxwell girl?" she asked abruptly.

I must have paused with confusion a moment, and she

45

seemed to draw back a little, more into the shadows. She was big, even taller than I, and well past middle age. She seemed to have dressed hastily, with something dark and shapeless thrown around her shoulders and her hair concealed under a wide-brimmed plastic rain hat that almost hid her broad, plain face.

"I'm Chrys Clement," I corrected, trying to place her face. "I'm Mr. Maxwell's granddaughter."

"You was out at Corners West," she said firmly.

I studied her warily. "This afternoon," I said. "I stopped for some Coke."

"You wasn't after Coke," she shook her head. "You was asking about Mathew."

"I did ask," I admitted, feeling suddenly very alone in the darkness with her. "Mr. Martin said he had no son."

"He'd say that," she said angrily. "It's his way. He holds grudges."

There was an awkward silence between us. I stood stubbornly waiting. This call had been her initiative, and anyway, there wasn't anything logical for me to say.

"Were you the girl?" she asked. "The one he was so took with?"

I shook my head, but she ignored it.

"It figures," she said to herself thoughtfully. "Money, class, he liked that." Suddenly her hand caught my arm. Her voice was tight with emotion. "Do you ever hear anything . . . why he left or anything?"

"No," I said honestly. "That's why I came to ask you today."

She shook her head. "He was gone just like that . . . no word to anyone. He even left with wages due him, because the man he worked for sent them along to us in care of the store after a week or two. You would have thought he'd have left a note for me, anyway. We was close, really close."

46

She paused and frowned deeply in the dim light. "There was something mysterious about him from the start, you know. We got checks. Every month by the tenth there was this check, always a bank draft with no signature, just made out to my old man. But when Mathew was gone a while the money stopped, just like the bank knew that he was gone. Old Martin took a grudge from that. He won't let the boy's name be mentioned even . . . hasn't for years."

"And you never knew where he went, or why?"

She shook her head. "I figure maybe it was a fit of temper over his girl," she stared at me searchingly a moment and then went on. "But when the time stretched on, that didn't seem reasonable. And I never heard direct for a long time."

She glanced about as if she were afraid someone were listening. "Cards came. Old Martin might have get some I didn't see, but they was from the Far East with funny stamps and always just a scrawled something, like 'best wishes,' and no signature at all. I figured it to be Mat, and I worried that he might be hurt or killed with the war and all."

She paused. "Then he came. Right soon after Christmas this year. He didn't come to the store—he sneaked around kind of and caught me on a trip into town." She smiled. "It wasn't much of a visit. He told me he had made it safe through the war and thought a lot about how good I'd been to him and wanted me to know. He brought me a piece of jewelry . . . jade he called it, real pretty. Not that I could ever wear it, but I keep it hid and look at it when I get to thinking on those times."

"Then he left again?" I asked.

She nodded. "Right off, I guess. But we talked a lot. He asked me about news, hometown news, you know. He seemed awful interested in the mill fire and how old Mr. Lyons got caught in that accident. Just gossip. But so big he had got,

47

such a fine man to have grown from such a slip of a boy."

"Are you his mother?" I asked gently.

When she ducked her head like that, her face was wholly concealed from me. "He was the closest I ever come to mothering," she said defensively. "He was only a tad when they brought him to us."

"Who brought him to you?" I asked quietly.

"A man," she said slowly. "A man I never saw before or since. I got the feeling he was from away. And there were papers to sign, and old Martin would have never let me take him to raise except that there was going to be this money from the bank regular every month till the boy was grown, and old Martin is money hungry."

"And you never even tried to check at the bank?"

"Oh, it wasn't this bank here," she said as if surprised. "It was from a big New York bank, likely we'd ever get to New York for anything."

There was a choked silence before her eyes raised to mine. I was suddenly stunned by her look of aching loneliness.

"If you meet up with him," she said slowly, "tell him I remember. Tell him I appreciate his remembering with the cards. Tell him how much his coming back meant to me.

"I'll always remember," she added after a minute.

Her eyes held mine only a moment more. Then she turned and bolted down the drive, a large woman with long, heavy strides. I listened to the motor of the truck choke to life, then roar as it jerked off down the street. I felt curiously empty.

I was soggy with soup and sleep when the phone rang about nine. It was Emily Lord.

"I have a passion for finishing things," she said abruptly. "I kept remembering about that Mathew Martin during dinner. Good-looking kid—tall and almost too good-looking

48

to be a boy. But what I wanted to tell you is that he and Mel had a thing on . . . one of those book-carrying, hand-holding, eyes-locked-in-the-library things. I don't know if they ever dated actually, since she was a freshman his junior year, but Mel might know more about him than anyone else."

I set the phone back in its cradle gently.

My search for Mathew Martin was starting badly—a fragment here, a shattered corner there, a world of dead ends—but San Francisco kept being the place all the signs pointed towards.

5

MISS TRU

Nothing and everything had changed back at college. The same naked poplars marched along snow-stained drives; reddened ivy rattled as drily as ever against the cold brick face of the dorm.

My own room greeted me as a stranger. The blazing poster sun that grinned widely above the plaid bedspread was somehow an affront to me. In five short weeks I had lost contact with the Chrys Clement whose reference books staggered between twin bronze statues along the back of the cluttered desk, and whose clothes, smelling faintly of winter dampness, hung limp and disconsolate on tired hangers.

I gave it a try. I really did give it an honest try; but nothing worked for me. No matter how purposefully I took myself in hand, muttering precepts of determination and perseverance, I could not lift my eyes from a page without my mind carrying me instantly back to Prathersville. The search for Mathew Martin hung in a waiting silence in my head.

It didn't help that I couldn't make any of the puzzle shake together into any form. A slow kind of seething anger built up in me from the frustration of all my unproductive musing. I was trying to assemble a whole man from a shattered bone or two dug from a silty cliff—and I am no paleontologist.

What facts did I really have? A man, now about thirty, had disappeared for no apparent reason right before his senior year in high school. (That was pegged as the year of the big mill fire, so it had to be 1959.) He was tall, handsome, clever with words, and was either an adopted or foster child to an angry old man and his semiliterate wife.

He had been a childhood sweetheart of Mel Lyons. So?

Maybe he had gone to war, and maybe he had come back.

Maybe. Maybe. Maybe. I plodded endless distracted circles from the dorm to the library and to class and back to the dorm.

Spring was coming to the Midwest. Naked tips of crocus pushed up among the tangled roots of matted grass. The willows were turning that brilliant yellow, which would later be covered with green. Overhead the haunting pilgrimage of migrations was angling its way across the sky.

A restless sense of urgency grew in me with every passing week. I must have subconsciously been looking for a reason to escape . . . any excuse to escape the remainder of that college term and try to knit together the dangling threads of the mystery of Mathew Martin.

My "way out" came almost as an aside in a letter from Vinnie. After two weeks visiting a relative in Daytona Beach, she had returned to keep Grand's great empty house tidy and her ear to the grapevine the way she always did.

Her letters were as stylized as sonnets. They opened with

a weather report ("moist under foot and the winter wheat already green"), moved on to the local gossip, and then to a cautionary close, reminding me to get plenty of rest and eat right. Her letters were always signed with the cheerful abbreviation: "Aff. Vinnie."

A small entry in the gossipy middle of her letter gave me the excuse I had been looking for.

> Ran into Corby Lyons at the market Tuesday. He has just had some terrible news of Miss Tru. Seems someone broke into her place out there, gave her a sharp lick on the head, and rifled the house and tried to set it on fire. Lucky somebody called the firemen before the place caught hold, but she was hurt bad, almost killed. According to Corby her skull was fractured and her collar bone broke, and she'll be in a hospital a long time . . . a kind of convalescent place they moved her to after the surgery was all over and she was past the big danger. Poor old thing. Makes a body wonder what the world is coming to when ruffians go after old folks who never bother a soul. The police are on it of course, but you know how those things are, half the time it takes forever and they still don't know a thing.
>
> I couldn't help thinking about Ambrose burning to death in that mill. Makes me think of Himself and how he talked about the Gods and all. But fortune would have it different for her, thank the Lord.

My decision was instantaneous.

I checked out. It was so simple that it scared me a little to realize that I really was accountable to no one. I simply packed my things off home, wrote Vinnie that I had decided to go out and help Miss Tru, and notified Mr. McAllister of my plans.

The last step of my arrangements was my letter to Miss Tru. Amazingly, that was the easiest one of all to write. I simply pretended I was Miss Tru herself and phrased it in that direct way she always expressed herself:

> I just heard about your awful invasion and I'm just sick about it. It's obvious that you need someone out there who gives a damn about you. Since that is me, I am on my way. I will be at the St. Francis Hotel in San Francisco by the time you get this. Please contact me so I can accept your invitation, which you can't back out of now.
> Take care and my Love.

I signed it Chryseis . . . the name my grandfather had chosen for me. He and Miss Tru are the only people who have ever called me that, except total strangers who always manage to stumble over the pronunciation.

After I finished the letter, I sealed it and sat there a long time just tapping it against my hand and thinking. Perhaps I should wait and mail it after I had a few days for my search for Mathew Martin. But Miss Tru would be acute enough to realize that it had been mailed in California, not from the Midwest. Anyway, being Miss Tru, she might even have known Mathew Martin and be able to help.

The last thing I did before boarding the plane for San Francisco was to post Miss Tru's letter. Only after we were skyborne and wheeling West did I have time or wit enough to entertain any serious doubts about this new adventure I had undertaken.

No matter how much I cherished Miss Tru, I am no nurse. Worse than that, thanks to Vinnie's efficiency and my boarding-school life, I am not even a borderline competent in a kitchen.

I tried to picture myself trying to nurse a seriously injured old woman back to health while searching for a half-imagined wraith of a lost young man.

53

I could be opening myself a veritable Pandora's box of troubles. I grinned out at the wide prairies below the plane. The very name of Pandora evoked the bookshelf in my room at home in Prathersville, with the handsome collection of Greek myths that Grand had given me long before I was old enough to hold *any* books.

Now its spine is frayed and faded to a neutral gray from its original deep, rich blue; its pages are spotted and crumbling at the edges from constant and careless use. But I know every picture in that book by heart, as well as most of the stories.

I thought of the illustration for "Pandora's Box" as I stared out that plane window. I could see the miasma of horrifying monsters moving in the shifting forms of the clouds below me, those monstrous evils that had risen like a legion of furies from the opened chest.

But in the end there was hope, I reminded myself sternly. In the end there was the small elfin tapping of hope, which was the last to be released.

I closed my eyes determinedly. Whatever rivers had passed beneath the moving plane, one of them for me had certainly been the Rubicon—and there was no turning back.

It was raining the first time I saw San Francisco. Water tunneled down the streets, and a great fog bank lay along the line of the sea. Gulls driven low by the storm swayed over the traffic moving up the peninsula into town.

The cabby was genial.

"First trip?" he asked, as I stared curiously through the streaming windows.

"The very first," I replied absently.

"Holiday or school break?" he asked.

I shook my head. He frowned at me in the rear-view mirror. He had a broad, crinkly face fringed by red hair.

"You're not another one of them runaways?" he asked sceptically.

I laughed as he drew up before the St. Francis and totaled his fare.

"Not hardly," I said, distracted with getting my change out. "I am looking for a man."

He sat my bags on the curb with a grin that went from sideburn to sideburn. "At last I have met an honest woman," he said. "I'll put a star on my calendar."

I grinned back at his open smile and the nice straight way he looked at me.

"Hey," I said thoughtfully. "Seriously. If there was a friend of yours that you thought was in this town but you didn't know how to reach him, how would you begin?"

He cocked his head a moment, then said, "I'd check the phone book of course, or maybe you could get a credit check on him. How old is he? Does he work?"

"About thirty," I said, "I'm not sure what he does."

"If he's got a job or ever bought a car, you can find him . . . anything on time, as a matter of fact," he shook his head. "But if he's gone hippie you might as well scrub it."

I nodded and added an extra dollar to the tip.

"Thanks for the advice."

"Any time," he grinned. "Good hunting!"

My first evening in everyone's dream city was a total bust. I wandered around Union Square under a freshly bought umbrella, got a bundle of flowers that didn't help brighten my room, had a lonely supper, and curled into bed disconsolately.

At least I had a plan. Part one of my great plan turned out to be no help at all. I checked the phone book and found no Mathew Martin with one *t*. I called the two M. Martins listed, and they turned out to be names that didn't fit and ages that were even further off base.

So part two would be the personals columns. I phrased two ads to place in the *Examiner* and *Chronicle*.

It was still early, and I felt a kind of loneliness that I didn't really understand. It was then that I called Mel. It was a funny conversation. An older woman answered and then called Mel to the phone. I'm not inclined to be suspicious, but I would have sworn that I heard another phone lift as I spoke to Mel.

"Are you already here, for heavens sake?" she asked with astonishment when I identified myself. "Auntie said you were coming."

"I'm here," I admitted cheerfully. "I decided to come out and see what I could do about helping Miss Tru out. I was kind of at loose ends, you know, after Grand . . ." My voice trailed off; I was caught with a surprise flood of emotion at the sound of his name in my voice.

"Oh, Chrys," she said quickly. "I was so sorry to hear. But let me come get you. We're free this evening. It's late but we could . . ."

"No, no, Mel," I protested quickly. "I have all these lags— jet and time and all that. I really just want to tuck in. I do need the number of Miss Tru's hospital so I can call her tomorrow."

"But you could stay with us," she argued. "We've tons of room."

"I honestly can't," I confessed. "I have another errand to perform—to look up a guy from Prathersville. I think I can best work from here until Miss Tru is ready to be dismissed."

"Maybe I can help," she suggested. "Is it anyone I'd know?"

"Only if you remember a Martin from Prathersville," I said frankly. "A Mathew Martin, in fact."

Her silence was overlong, and her voice, when it came again, was strangely cool and distant. "No bells ring," she said calmly, "and that is at least a common name. Let me get the number of Miss Tru's room for you. She has a private line, and you can call anytime tomorrow."

I shrugged as I reached for my pen. "Good try," I told myself. "Not productive, but a good try."

"Do promise me this," she said when she had recited the number to me. "We are going to go see her before dinner tomorrow night. Let's meet out there, and then you have dinner with Bran and me. I insist."

"I accept," I said quickly. "I'm so anxious to see you."

"Tomorrow about seven then?" she asked. "Can we pick you up?"

I barely hesitated. "No thanks," I said. "Heavens knows where I shall have wandered to on my quest by then. I'll meet you at the hospital."

"I'll look forward to that," she said, still cooly.

After she hung up I held the phone a moment, listening. I was right . . . two clicks. Someday I would tell her that she had a housekeeper without eavesdropping scruples, but for now I only shivered my way under the covers and lay there feeling strangely forlorn.

But there was tomorrow, I promised myself. Tomorrow the ads would go in, and the law of averages had to be with me if I kept trying . . . and kept trying and still kept on.

I pushed the light switch and tried to go to sleep. My mind drifted with the unfamiliar sounds of a hotel at night—the hum of the elevator, snatches of muffled conversations in the corridor outside, and the steady drumming of the rain against my draped windows.

PART TWO

The Knees of
the Gods

These things lie surely on the
knees of gods.

Homer

6

A BOX FOR
PANDORA

The storm had lifted by morning, and my spirits with it. I hummed as I dressed and lingered over the morning paper and the excellent croissants and coffee.

Somehow San Francisco stands tall in its sunlight. There was none of that sense of harried haste, of people bent by their world, which one feels in the streets of other large cities.

The girls all seemed threateningly beautiful and assured, and the crisp long-legged joviality of the men made my errands a positive pleasure.

With a nice brisk sense of achieving, I left the newspaper offices and started crosstown (if crosstown can mean straight up and down) to have my own private look at the city before I called Miss Tru.

That day was a strange experience for me. Goodness knows, I've done the tourist bit enough times, but never before had I done it alone.

I did a lot—the Fleischhacker Zoo, the Arboretum at Golden Gate Park, even tea for one in the Japanese Garden. I gawked at Coit Tower and Grace Cathedral and wandered tiredly through the shops in Chinatown. I would have bought a wok for Vinnie but couldn't figure out how to send it home with any ease.

So I settled on postcards and retreated to the peace of my hotel room. Somewhere in the zoo I had plucked a wad of leaves and a strange pod from a tree. I only caught at it absentmindedly and didn't notice the strange odor until I was stretched out on my bed in the hotel room.

Gradually the room was filled with a curious pervasive odor that seemed to come from some long-ago time.

I needed to call Miss Tru. Instead I lay and probed for what scent it was that had thrown me back so many years.

When it came to me, I retrieved the pod and the leaves from my jacket pocket and collapsed on the bad with gales of laughter. Whatever that tree was, it smelled of Celeste Lammers, with whom I had shared a room during my seventh grade at school.

I studied the pod a long time. I had never seen one shaped like that before. It was rather like an acorn cup with a serrated rim, except that there was no depression in it large enough to hold any possible acorn. Even the slightest scrape of my thumbnail strengthened the medicinal smell that "was" Celeste.

I could actually see her thin, pale face framed by limp, pale hair, her skinny legs and knobby knees that the sturdiest of stockings could not disguise.

And her sniffle!

I roomed with Celeste for nine interminable months, during which she was never without complaint. Her autumn respiratory problems worsened into a winter cold, which was only displanted by the onset of her spring allergies. She never could speak to me until she shifted a lozenge to one cheek, like a half-stuffed chipmunk.

It was that smell, the constant cough-drop smell, that had clung to Celeste at all seasons that now giddied my head as I pressed the slender leaves between my fingers.

My case of childish giggles had somehow restored my energy, and I dialed the number that Mel had given me. On the third ring, Miss Tru's brusque voice snapped a sharp greeting at me.

"Where in the name of God have you been all day?" she asked after a moment. "Mel called me and told me where you were, and I've rung the ear off that hotel operator ever since."

"Prowling," I admitted. "I didn't want to spoil your day too early."

"Spoil my day, indeed!" she snorted, and then she laughed.

"You crazy child! What ever got into you to come honking out here for an old hellion like me? But am I ever glad you did!" In her disorganized way she chattered on, as I gradually relaxed and pitched myself across the bed to listen to her ramblings.

Finally, I got in an edgewise question of my own.

"Tell me about all this. Do the police have any leads or anything?"

"Not really," she said quietly, a difference of fear in her voice that I had never heard before. "I thought the house was locked tight, but I must have missed something, because there was no sign of a break-in. I was full of wine, so it was easy enough to bonk me on the head and go through the place. I guess it was the fire that saved me. Whoever it was set the drapes on fire and they smoldered, being specially treated. Luckily somebody sent a report in time, and they got me to the hospital."

"Had you had any strange people around, loiterers or anything?" I asked, remembering Vinnie's repeated warning back home.

"No," the answer came hesitantly. "Not really anyone with a reason."

"Well," I sighed, "I sacrifice a fat lamb to Zeus that you were saved."

After a small silence she spoke again. "It's you all right, Chryseis. And I am on the mend. In the meantime, there's no call for you to mope around that hotel. I've stuck my house and car keys in an envelope here for you. If you aren't petrified of California drivers, you can do me a favor by keeping my battery up, as well as have wheels of your own.

"Oh, and Chryseis," she added, "I always collect what my family calls funny friends! I have a gardener friend that comes and goes. If you see him, tell him I'd sure appreciate his keeping things from getting out of hand. The police haven't seen him around, but he might turn up. When will I see you?"

"How about tonight?" I asked.

"I was hoping you would ask," she laughed. "Visitors welcome from seven until eight-thirty. But this place is clear to hell and gone from Union Square."

"I didn't come clear out here to be deterred by a mile or two," I reminded her. "Can I bring you anything?"

She laughed. "A decent bottle of wine might be nice," she said kiddingly. "The house wine in this miserly ménage is watered-down tea. They even toss salads with it."

I was humming to myself as I walked through the hotel lobby. Just the sound of Miss Tru's voice had restored my confidence. It was beautiful.

64

I had passed the desk when the clerk called me back. "Miss Clement," he said briskly, "I have a message for you."

Startled, I returned and accepted the small card he handed me from the key slot. I stopped to read it. It was a small informal note with Brandon North engraved elegantly across the front. The note was simple: "We are looking forward to dinner with you tonight with greatest anticipation." It was signed, Mel and Bran.

It was a thoughtful gesture, and I reread the note with a feeling somewhat like flattered pleasure.

I waited outside for only a moment or two before the doorman hailed a cab for me.

The cab driver smiled contentedly when I gave him the address of the hospital. He flipped the flag like he was opening a Christmas present. "So it's only money," I told myself airily as he eased out into the fog that shrouded Union Square.

The fog thinned as we moved south.

Then, strangely, the cabby caught my eye in the mirror and asked mildly, "Somebody bird-dogging you?"

I stared at him. "I guess I don't know what you mean," I confessed.

"We picked up a car about a block from the hotel, and he's following us," he said.

"But that's ridiculous," I said. "Why should anyone follow me?"

"They sure aren't following *me*," he pointed out. "Want me to prove it?"

"Sure," I challenged, "if you can."

He made several right turns so that we described a large square. It must have encompassed sixteen blocks.

When we returned to the original point, the same set of

headlights was following us a discreet half block back. It gave me an eerie, invaded feeling that I didn't like.

"Now you believe?" he asked.

"I believe," I said half angrily.

"Want to lose him?" he asked casually, with a hint of boyish mischief in his voice.

I stared at him a moment thoughtfully. If somebody was following me, they deserved more than just getting lost.

"I'd love to . . . if you can."

"Sure I can," he said confidently. "Anyone of a half-dozen ways."

He left the main drag and wound up into a hilly residential district. He chatted companionably as we wove in and out, always with the lights of the blue Ford just a block or two behind.

"Used to do a lot of this in the old days . . . before the divorce laws were updated. Considered myself a little of a specialist. Let's do it the classy way tonight, okay?"

"Anything you say," I answered, restraining myself from perching forward on the seat like a kid. I was halfway ashamed of being so childish. Whatever reason the man had for following me, it had to be serious. But the cabby's playfulness had infected me, and I was having a glorious time.

The neighborhood got steadily better. One after another we passed huge estates with magnificent gardens and stunning lighting effects that accented their splendor. The cab driver slowed down, as if searching for a house number. As we followed a wide curve, we came upon an immense house lit for a party. Mark IVs and Mercedes sedans punctuated the Cadillacs along the street. My cab pulled into the circular drive slowly, and the driver gave me instructions. "I'll stop at the doorway, get out, and open your door. You pretend to pay me, and while I'm going around to the other side, you slide down in the floor of the backseat. Then I'll take off, and it will look like I'm alone."

I have never felt quite so ridiculous in my life. A dignified Oriental man in black was admitting guests at the door as the cab drew up. He gave me a cursory glance, turned towards the inner hall, and then looked back towards the drive where I should have been. I was gone. I caught only his astonished gaze as he watched the cab pulling away, the driver making a great thing of using his car radio as if to check the next call.

"How long do I stay down?" I asked in a whisper.

"Maybe a block or two," he suggested. "He's probably parked there to wait, but there is no point in taking chances. Nice party you missed, wasn't it?"

I giggled. "They looked too old for me," I admitted, "and too rich. How did you know there would be a party there?" I asked curiously.

"There's always a big one somewhere," he said airily. "I was prepared to shop around. It's your meter, you know."

At eight o'clock sharp he let me out at the door of the hospital. I raced through the lobby almost at a run. Miss Tru had said the visiting hours ran to eight-thirty, and that didn't give me much time with her.

When I reached the second floor, the hall seemed to stretch like an ill-lit tunnel ahead of me. Doors stood ajar along its length, fanning angles of light into the dimness of the hall. From identical beds in identical rooms, strangely identical faces stared back at me as I searched for room twenty-three.

The rooms seemed emptied of life, even though they were filled with people. The glances from the beds seemed to light on me vacantly, before sliding on to some darkness beyond my face.

Room twenty-three offered a startling contrast. The windowsills were banked with flowers, and against their brightness stood a slender woman in evening dress.

She was so beautiful that I stood a moment just staring at her. Her perfect body was draped in a deep emerald green that clung to her slenderness before swirling about dark evening sandals.

Strangely, something about her echoed the same lifeless apathy that had struck me along the hospital corridor. With her expressionless mouth and heavy-lashed eyes, she seemed like something frozen into a doomed waiting.

I must have gasped for she turned her glance towards me, without emotion or interest. As she did so, Miss Tru gave a cry from her bank of pillows, and a man rose abruptly, scraping a chair harshly in the silence.

But I had trouble pulling my attention from Mel. It was weird how little she had changed, looking no older than she had at twelve and in the same instant, no younger than eternity.

"There you are," Miss Tru cried with relief. "My God, I thought you'd been swallowed up by something."

I went swiftly to the bed to embrace her. Her face felt cool and crisp against my cheek, and her hand gripped mine in a spasm of relief.

"Nothing so dire," I laughed, and turned to Mel.

"How lovely you look, Mel," I said genuinely. "And how good to see you."

There was a cool wariness in her greeting that disconcerted me. "I don't think you've ever met Bran," she replied, turning her eyes swiftly from me to him. "Chrys, this is my husband, Brandon North."

Brandon North is not a big man, but he has a presence that makes him fill more space in a room than he really claims physically. In spite of the wings of gray at his temple and a slenderness in his face, he looked younger than I expected, probably because of his eyes. His gaze was almost like a child's—open and direct with a kind of expectant curiosity. He caught my hand in both of his, and his voice was warm with greeting.

"At last I meet the fabled Chrys," he said, as if this had been something he had anticipated breathlessly. "So you're Jackson Maxwell's granddaughter!"

"And Sylvia's child," Mis Tru put in quietly. "You must remember Sylvia."

His glace slid to her and then back to me. "Could anyone ever forget Sylvia?" he bantered.

"It must be tiresome to be the daughter of a famed beauty," Mel said quietly.

I felt awkward and disoriented. There were currents of meaning in the room that I wasn't getting. But Bran's famous charm came on with such force that the conversation stabilized into channels I could at least handle.

"We were all worried about you, Chrys," he kidded. "We raced out here on the dot and started our vigil. Then, when you *didn't* arrive . . ." his voice trailed off almost in a question.

I slid into the chair Bran offered me and lied glibly, without compunction. "I ran into an old friend . . . and time just got away."

"Now, don't tell me it was someone from Prathersville," he laughed.

"I won't," I grinned at him. "I have a bare handful of friends from there, and two of them are in this room."

"I was sorry to hear about your grandfather, Chrys," Mel broke in, as if the conversation had suddenly gotten out of hand. She had still not moved from her post by the window. Her immobility seemed as tense as it was graceful.

"Thank you, Mel," I said, feeling strangely stilted. "Your flowers were lovely, and we very much appreciated them."

69

"We decided you must be angry at us," Bran said reproachfully. "Having to find out you were here only by chance through your letter to Auntie."

"It was a quick decision," I explained. "I got this overwhelming impulse to come out and bully Miss Tru while she was unable to defend herself."

Bran laughed gaily. "It's high time someone turned those tables on her. But you must come and stay with us until she is able to come home. A hotel is no place for a girl like you."

"Chryseis has some business of her own to do," Mel said quietly. "By the time she finishes that, Miss Tru will be able to go home too."

"That's a pity." Bran's disappointment seemed genuine. "We have loads of room, and the weather is much better where we are."

At the sound of a thin bell from the hall outside, Miss Tru emitted a muffled curse. She opened the drawer of her bedside table and fished about in it. With a strange shock of recognition, I noticed a notebook—an "exercise book" they were always called at school—a slender book of a deep tan mottled color. It struck me that it must be the journal that Miss Tru had faithfully kept all these years. She must be keeping it even here in the eventless cloister of a hospital room. She pulled an envelope, which I assumed contained the house and car keys, from the drawer, then scribbled something on a memo sheet and tucked it inside. As she handed it to me she nodded towards Bran, "Some little jobs to keep Chrys out of mischief."

"I hope I do better at this than at getting you the wine," I laughed. "They have a funny rule about being twenty-one."

Bran ignored my kidding. He frowned almost as if he were hurt. "If there is anything you need, Auntie, you should let Mel and me take care of it for you." His tone was almost cross. "We mustn't worry our guest with it."

70

"She's the only one who knows exactly what I want," Miss Tru said tartly. "Anyway, it's the only way I can be sure she gets out here to see me every day." She winked at him as she said it.

"*You* are the obstinate one," he sighed, rising to help Mel into her wrap. "That bell means eviction, Chrys. Wish you could join us, Auntie."

"I've had my pabulum and cardboard, thank you," she said with a wry smile.

"Very well, old girl." He leaned and kissed Miss Tru heartily on the forehead. "Behave yourself and get out of that cast—it's not your best color."

She grinned at him and caught my hand. "See you tomorrow?"

"For longer . . . I promise," I told her and followed them out.

That dinner with Mel and Bran was like a series of vignettes unified only by the smooth charm of Bran's manner. Miss Tru was right, he is an irresistible guy, a good listener and warmly anticipatory of every mood. Mel, so quiet and withdrawn, was obviously the golden apple of his eye, and his gallantry towards her was touching.

We dined at a place on Post called the Ritz Old Poodle Dog. I glanced about at the dining room, feeling awfully underdressed for the decor—panels of dark wood and ruby-red damasks, great deep mirrors catching the light of brilliant candelabra.

"It's rather something, isn't it?" Bran said disarmingly. "It's a real affectation for immigrants like us, but we always like the the oldest San Francisco places the best. This one dates from 1849 . . . on a different street but the first of the Poodles."

"It's lovely," I said.

After lauding the skills of the chef, Bran ordered excellent escargots, a Caesar salad, and chicken for the three of us. The entrée was delicious, sautéed and served with a sauce that was subtle with mushrooms and wine. The wild rice was incredible.

"Someday you must join us here for the sole," he chattered, keeping talk alive in spite of Mel's silence. For I still hadn't talked to Mel. Somehow the conversation rippled and spun around us, as if Bran and I were the old friends and Mel the relative stranger. I felt disoriented and a little depressed, as if I were being made into something different from myself by this warm man's obvious desire to give me a good time and make me feel at home.

And I kept hearing my own concern, like a slow bell ringing in the back of my head. "Something is wrong with Mel . . . something is terribly wrong with Mel."

When the meal was finally over, Bran went for the car. Mel huddled in her floor-length cape as if trying to retreat. Then she suddenly looked very straight at me and asked in that low, soft voice.

"Are you serious about what you said this afternoon, Chrys? That you're looking for someone?"

I nodded. "But it doesn't matter if you don't remember him."

We had only a second. Bran was pulling the Citroen into the curb and would be with us instantly.

"I remember nothing," she said calmly. "I remember nothing and no one." It was as if a curtain had fallen between us and her voice were coming through it, muffled and indistinct.

"I remember nothing," she said with finality. "I had no life before Bran. There was no Prathersville for me, no one before that. I began all over again. That's why Bran is so kind to me, you see. I am really a child—with no memories."

My simile had been weak. It was not a curtain, it was a

door that Mel was closing purposefully between us. "Prathersville does not exist for me . . . there was no one before Bran." I was a part of that past that she had closed her consciousness to.

I shivered a little as the Citroen slid smoothly into the curb, and Bran came around swiftly to hold the door for Mel.

Mel's hand rested lightly on his arm, and she smiled at him, a shadow of a smile that somehow didn't make it to her eyes. He put me in beside her. "It's cozier," he said. But there was nothing cozy about Mel's slender stiffness beside me on the seat.

Bran would have seen me clear into the lobby of my hotel, but I protested. He stood outside the car, holding my hand in parting.

"You can't know how glad I am," he said earnestly, "to meet a good friend from those other years of Melanie's. She's never really gotten over the fire and her father's death. You sensed that, I guess."

His face was dark with concern. "But maybe from whatever place your early friendship came, a new one can come . . . don't you think that's possible?"

"It would be nice," I replied without conviction.

Numbly, my mind full of Melanie and her effusive husband, I took an elevator up to my room.

7

A SMALL TAPPING
LIKE HOPE

All I knew about Sunday was that I didn't want to spend any of it with Bran and Mel. Yet it lay there before me when I wakened, a huge hopscotch square between myself and the day that I might get some first response to my ads.

I called Miss Tru at the earliest possible moment. We chatted a while, and I told her that I was going to spend the day sight-seeing.

"I may eat all of the five cuisines of Chinatown before I'm through," I told her, "but I will be there with you at the hospital at the dot of seven."

"I'll have the milk of magnesia ready," she replied thoughtfully. "It's a great idea . . . and have a good day."

The day did start well enough with a leisurely breakfast in the little Dutch coffee shop downstairs.

74

But something seemed to change when I left the hotel. I went to The Cannery and Fisherman's Wharf. I caught a ferry to Tiburon and prowled the shops along Main Street. The day was beautiful, clear, and bright, and warm enough to carry my blazer most of the time. But something had changed, and I could not pin down in my mind what it was.

But always I had the curious feeling that I was never quite alone. Even on the ferry passing Alcatraz on the open bay, watching brown pelicans dive at their fantastic angles for fleeing fish, it had always seemed that if I glanced about quickly and knew just where to look, I would surprise some secret companion stalking me.

It was an eerie, unsettling feeling that robbed my day of pleasure.

I was afraid. I was afraid even to admit to myself I was afraid. But slowly I had, in this area of warm friendly people, begun to feel the growing tension of someone always watching me. And waiting.

It was ridiculous. When I returned to the familiar confines of my hotel room in the late afternoon, I convinced myself that I was being a silly school girl squeaking at shadows. But when I thought of going out again, the memory of that feeling haunted me until I gave up, resigned myself to the solitary comforts of book and television, and waited for the time for my evening call on Miss Tru.

That was a good evening we spent together. Fortunately, Mel and Bran had some social engagement, and Miss Tru and I giggled and gossiped about Prathersville and my grandfather and avoided with mutual delicacy the awkwardness of the evening before. She talked a lot more about her house on the hill, about the birds that wintered in her garden and reeled drunkenly about when the pyracantha berries became a little high proof for their constitutions. The

75

hour and a half sped so quickly that I couldn't believe it when the small warning bell rang in the hall for the visitors to leave.

Somehow I had forgotten the note she had given me the night before. We didn't mention the keys either—I guess she must have understood that I would use them when I felt the need.

I wouldn't look out the back of the cab that took me home. I didn't want to know if I was being followed again. Tomorrow was Monday, and in spite of myself I had put a ridiculous amount of faith in the ads that had now run long enough to elicit at least some response.

Response there certainly was. I excitedly returned to the hotel with a healthy packet of envelopes in my purse and an unreasoning anticipation towards opening them.

My spirits fell steadily as I poured through the carefully slit envelopes one by one.

After reading them I sorted them methodically into little heaps.

The expression, "in relation to an estate," seemed to have triggered most of the responses. There were crank notes and letters of supplication, one rambling letter about an elderly man by the name of Martin whom the writer had known years before in Daly City, and then a large legal-sized white envelope with no return address. Inside, on a folded file card in bold block letters, was printed a phone number and then, in parentheses, "after five only."

I am the world's worst waiter. Waiting for anyone or anything is quite beyond me, and the weekend just past had worn down my patience to a ragged shred.

I wandered out on Union Square, found a needlework shop and browsed through knitting books until I found a bedjacket pattern that would possibly work for Miss Tru. The clerk stiffened with disapproval when I bought the most outrageous shade of shocking pink she had in stock. I had the advantage on her. I *knew* Miss Tru.

I had cast on the back and had the pattern well-established by the time that the dawdling clock finally reached four-thirty. I started calling the number at five-minute intervals.

Finally, a little after five, my persistence was rewarded. The young, strong male voice that answered was a little hostile even in greeting.

"I am calling about Mathew Martin," I said directly.

"So?" he asked bluntly.

"The ad in the paper," I explained. "Someone sent this number to me in reply to my ad in the paper."

"I guess I wasn't expecting a woman," he said grudgingly. "You are looking for Mathew Martin?"

"I am," I replied.

"Why?" he came back curtly.

"Like the ad says, I need to contact him about some property in an estate. Who are you?"

"A friend," he said, then added, "a close friend."

"He's fine," he said in an ironic tone. "The best of health . . ."

"I don't mean that," I interrupted almost crossly. "Tell me so that I will know that we are talking about the same man."

He paused a moment, then began slowly. "Only child . . . Prathersville, Indiana . . . four years in the Navy . . . dark hair, blue eyes . . . anything else?"

I was having a hard time keeping my voice level.

"That's fine," I said slowly. "But I need to see him . . . myself."

"You'll have to see me first," he said.

"How will I know that you . . ." My voice trailed off. What had I meant to ask? If he could really help me . . . ? If he actually knew where Mathew Martin was . . . ? The questions were rhetorical. I was in no position to quibble. "Tell me what you have in mind," I finished lamely.

"We could meet," he said brusquely. "Some place convenient and public, and talk."

Why was he so wary? What was Mathew Martin hiding from?

"You know this city better than I," I said. "Name the place."

"How about the fountain on Ghirardelli Square at six-thirty this evening?"

"That's fine," I agreed quickly. "I'm tall and dark-haired and will be wearing a yellow raincoat."

"You'll probably need it," he said curtly and hung up.

A ridiculous feeling of elation filled me. I had a wild urge to race right over to Ghirardelli Square and wait there for the next hour and a half. Maybe the search for Mathew Martin was really going to be over. Probably this friend of Mathew Martin's only wanted money, and that should be no problem. Then he would put me in touch with Martin himself, and my promise to Grand would be fulfilled—I would gain a certain peace that I had not really had since Grand's death.

After the Mathew Martin thing was over, things would be different. I would move into Miss Tru's hill house and get it all ready for her return. Maybe I could even practice cooking so I could do a better job with Miss Tru. It was enough that someone knew where Mathew Martin was, and I was meeting him in less than two hours.

I was too excited for anything so humdrum as knitting. I paced about the room and then fell back on the classic female stratagem for passing time. After an oil bath, I read and did my nails while my hair dried. The clock hands stirred sluggishly to six, and finally, my heart beating faster than I could ever remember, I swung through the doors of the St. Francis and onto a cable car.

It was the beginning of the end, and the cable car ride felt like a roller coaster—just fun and the wind swift through my hair.

The rain of the past days had cleansed the bay and the hills so that they gleamed with color. I was only a few minutes early—not enough time to wander through the shops and finger the tempting displays. "Later," I promised myself happily. I went straight to the fountain and took my station there, belting my coat tightly against the chill breeze and the spray of the fountain.

I watched a bevy of sailboats, each punctuated by a single scarlet spinnaker, executing turns like uncertain dancers choreographed by the wind. Fisherman's Wharf hummed with bodies.

People flowed along the sidewalks past the fishing boats, which nudged the redolent docks. The idle, almost lazy motion of the boats contrasted dramatically with the crowds of tourists that seemed driven by some frantic, hidden force. Their faces were stamped with the frenzy of dwindling time.

Below me at the base of the steps, a quartet of street musicians executed Haydn with surprising delicacy. But none of the tourists had time to fish for a coin or pause for an obbligato.

I thought about the game we sometimes managed to play when I was boarding at St. Mary's. Crack the Whip, we called it. Looking like a string of identical cut-out paper dolls in our uniforms, we swung each other around in faster and faster circles. The ones at the end, fighting to hang on, were inevitably thrown loose by a force that we would only understand and be able to name much later in a physics class. Of course we were never allowed to play the game when the sisters were watching.

"Someone could be thrown against the wall," Sister Theresa had squeaked in agitation while she pulled our hands apart, as if she could foil disaster by isolating those clinging hands from each other. "You could be killed . . . even killed."

The swaying crowds along the wharf and around the Square were being flung loose. No matter how hard they clung or how fast they ran, they were doomed to be thrown back into the lives they had fled from . . . to be harried by crabgrass and frozen windshields and the numbing routine of their jobs . . . leaving San Francisco to gleam and preen in the mirrors of her bay.

I shivered and stirred a little to move from the spray that had fastened wet strands of my hair against my face. I turned my coat collar a little higher against the coolness of the rising wind and buried my hands deeper into my pockets. I frowned at the clock. He was late. Whoever had answered that phone so crossly and set this date was already late. I shifted my weight to brace against the tired child who was dragged by me, whimpering with exhaustion and sticky with treats.

I couldn't admit to myself that possibly he wouldn't come at all. He had been so strange, so prickly and devious. But he was still the only viable link I had to Mathew Martin, and he absolutely had to come.

Past the fragrance of chilies and onion that drifted from Senor Pico's, past the bookstore with its browsing natives, to the man in the doorway of the flower stall. He was slender and anonymous and middle-aged. He occasionally peered myopically around the square, only to lapse into an almost houndlike attitude of resignation. His feet were set widely apart as if to support him for all time—for a forever if necessary—while the crowd shoved by him and on past me on their covetous errands.

I noticed that once in a while he gazed idly past the crowds that jostled the street musicians, towards the steps

80

that led down to the bay. Another man stood there on the steps, listening to the music with a curious fixed expression, as if their strains moved over and about him without entering anywhere.

I asked myself if either of them could be the man who had called me, and decided they couldn't be. They were too old, for one thing. The voice on the phone had been that of a young, angry man—late twenties perhaps—and deep like the voice of a person who carries some weight.

Then I saw a young man crossing the square. When I stared at him he glanced away and stopped a minute to buy a chocolate bar at the booth across from the flower stall. He didn't have to be the right man, I told myself sternly. But there was something in the tension of his walk towards me that made my breath come a little quicker. If he was not my mysterious telephone caller, then I might just have a small confrontation to get through. But if he was the right man, the search might be nearing an end.

I watched him move towards me and felt a strange breathlessness. That eerie feeling that had followed me all weekend was stronger than ever before. "Oh, please be Mathew Martin's friend," I begged silently as I studied his approach.

8

A FACE LIKE
WALLPAPER

There was no sun on the flowers in the square now. Oakland, across the bay, gleamed in its last light like something ethereal and unreachable. It seemed to me that a special chillness of a shadow moved over me as the tall man approached. He was a big one, that was for sure, but he moved lightly on his feet with that kind of bounce that I always associate with really superb athletes. His hair was that combination of auburn with sun-bleached strands that suggested hours of being outside, and the darkness of the tan on his unsmiling face added to the effect.

Under ordinary circumstances I think I would have registered him as handsome, but the quickening in my breathing numbed my automatic responses. What struck me was that at his approach, not only I, but the whole scene seemed to have changed. The man by the flower stall, the one with the face as inconspicuous as wallpaper, suddenly looked alive and tense, as if he had been activated by some hidden current. It was like some scene in a slow-motion sequence, where ordinary things become extraordinary and somehow ominous. Inside my pocket, I turned a coin furiously between my fingers, as if polishing it would magically make this tall suntanned man turn into the friend of Mathew Martin whom I needed so badly to talk to.

There was a great deal of certainty in the tall young man's manner. He paused on the other side of the fountain, carefully peeled back his candy paper, and deposited it in a waste can before calmly starting to eat. Did I imagine that he glanced about almost casually before sauntering over to me?

Then suddenly, across the fountain from me, he raised his eyes to me, and his whole face changed instantly to a wide boyish grin. Quite loudly, as if he wished to be overheard, he cried out.

"Well, hey there!" He was instantly upon me, catching me by the shoulders and holding me tightly. "Doll!" he said happily as he brushed my cheek with an embrace. As his face touched mine, he spoke quickly. "Mathew Martin. Now act glad to see me . . . call me Rick."

"Rick," my voice squeaked with falsity as I struggled to free myself from his clutch. "Imagine!"

"You aren't waiting for someone, are you?" he asked, his voice a little too loud for civility.

His dark eyes held mine commandingly. I shook my head furiously, then paused. "I was, but I guess I've been stood up."

Why this ridiculous act? I could feel the stares of the passing crowd, and my helplessness with my arms trapped against my sides filled me with frustration. I was ready to throw off the whole scene and demand some sense from him, but he was too quick for me.

He caught my arm and swept me towards the stairs. "His loss is my gain. Come have a drink with me at Rolf's. Are you still working with Fennimore? And you've got to fill me in on Betty!"

Fennimore . . . Betty. I almost burst into laughter. What a ham! And for what reason?

While I was struggling for balance on the stairs and clinging tightly to his arm, he marched me across the street and made a sudden hard right into an import shop. He hustled me halfway back into the store, through air heavy with incense, and past loaded counters of bright merchandise that dazzled my eyes.

Suddenly he stopped and turned to stare at the windows facing the street. Then he turned to me as if satisfied.

"Now, take off that loud coat."

As I obeyed awkwardly, he took my raincoat and turned it inside out over his arm. Then we were off again, but not toward Rolf's. Indeed we were crossing the street against a stream of protesting traffic.

Past beds of drowsy flowers and over grass already wet with evening dew, he led me towards the turnaround spot for the cable car. A herd of baggage-laden shoppers had clustered there, but as the car began to load Rick shouldered me past them. Then, ignoring their outrage and voluble protests, he lifted me on.

I was pressed tightly against him on the outer bench before I finally caught my breath. The car had jerked to a start, and the bay dropped away behind us as I looked back.

"Now, where are we going?" I asked coldly, chilled without my coat and flustered from the manhandling I had taken.

"Nowhere yet," he said, as the car clicked up Powell Street towards Nob Hill.

"I can talk, can't I? I can ask questions?" I inquired acidly.

"If you must," he said absently, looking back towards the wharf area.

"Why all this cops and robbers?" I asked. "I want to see Mathew Martin, not do the tourist bit with you."

"I'm the only way you'll get to Martin," he said carefully, still not looking at me but straining about to examine the faces of the other passengers.

Then, unaccountably, he relaxed and turned to stare at me. "You're young," he said with obvious astonishment. "Why, you're no more than a kid." His voice was honest with surprise. "You don't really mind that I had to get rid of your friends?"

"Friends," I squeaked. "I don't even know what you're talking about."

"The bird dogs," he said impatiently. "I got there early and waited on the upper balcony. I saw you come, and right after, the two tails took up cover positions."

I stared at him. "You really saw them!" I said firmly. "I wasn't imagining them?"

He looked at me cynically. "They're not *my* friends," I protested. "I keep thinking there's someone, but I don't know who or why."

"Then a couple of bright eyes are sure working for nothing," he said caustically. "May I see that?" Without waiting for an answer, he took my purse and opened it casually.

I watched with growing anger as he explored my wallet. He nodded, "Chryseis Clement," he mumbled aloud, "Prathersville, Indiana." After studying my statistics and identification, he rummaged deeper into my purse.

"Surely that's enough," I said furiously, grabbing for it.

"Tell me about Prathersville," he commanded abruptly.

85

I stared at him unbelieving. But he was sincere. He really meant for me to go through an inquisition about my hometown.

"It's a small town, mostly agricultural," I began slowly. "About fifteen thousand people . . ."

"Industry?"

I shook my head. "Not really. There's always been a mill there . . . that's the closest." I groped in my mind. This was so ridiculous. "A bank," I said suddenly, "my grandfather's bank."

"His name?" he snapped.

"Maxwell," I said sulkily. "Jackson Lane Maxwell."

"And you grew up there?"

"Not really," I admitted. "Now listen . . ."

"This is important," he said warningly, interrupting me. "How come you say you're from there and you didn't grow up there?"

"My parents are both dead," I said icily, wondering if I would ever get over that funny tug I get when I have to say it out like that. "My grandfather raised me, but he sent me away to school. Now what in hell does this have to do with my seeing Mathew Martin?"

"I have to be sure you are on the level," he said flatly.

Even as we talked, his glance moved warily along the street, watching the traffic moving alongside us.

Suddenly he seemed obsessed by haste.

"If you're not the real thing, you sure have elaborate properties," he conceded.

The cable car crested at California Street, clanging its bell furiously to force a confused green sedan off the tracks. "Land of a Thousand Lakes," I read absently on the license plate above a dealer's tag from Duluth. Some guy from Duluth with a red-headed teen-ager doesn't believe that

86

cable cars always get the right-of-way. And this Rick is not only crazy, but he's trying to scare me to death!

Suddenly I felt the hotness of angry tears behind my eyes. The tension of the past few weeks came in on me like something heavy and soft, enveloping me. I ducked my head and swallowed hard to make my eyes behave. All those ridiculous hopes I had pinned on a call from a madman converged with my fatigue, and I fought for self-control.

As we began the descent towards Union Square, I could hear short intakes of breath from behind me in the car and a muted adolescent squeal. The fog must have started in from the sea. From the direction of the Golden Gate the low fog horn sounded its mournful vigilance above the clatter of the car and the voices of the other passengers.

"Look Clem," this "Rick" said to me tersely. "Like I said, you have great props. If you're not the real thing, I'll be cutting my limb off for good."

"My name is Chrys," I said coldly, but then I met his eyes. There was an inexpressible pleading in his dark eyes that gave me a sudden surge of guilt—guilt about something I didn't even understand. And the hurt of the guilt made me angry, "I don't get you at all," I said fiercely. "All I'm doing is looking for a guy because I have something that belongs to him that I promised to deliver. I don't know any reason anyone would want to follow me. I don't know why you are so damned paranoid. I only want to reach Mathew Martin and get through with this whole thing."

He watched me carefully. "Who else knows you are looking for Martin?" he asked.

I shrugged. "Nobody really. I couldn't find listings for him anywhere. I did ask an old friend from Prathersville, but she claims not even to remember him."

"Claims?" he asked warily.

"She's a funny girl," I said frankly. "And she's been away

so long that she has put all of that time . . . that town and everything out of her mind."

"But she's level?"

"She wouldn't have me followed, if that's what you mean. Why should she?"

He smiled a strange, humorless smile. "The wrong somebody knows you are looking for Martin, that's for sure. So you're into it . . . willy-nilly." He grinned a little wryly. "Miss Innocence of Prathersville, Indiana." He shook his head and sighed. Then his glance turned speculative. "If I decide you are on the level, where can you be reached?"

"At the St. Francis," I replied. "But only for a day or two more."

"And you are registered under this name?"

"It's my own name," I almost shouted at him.

"All right, Clem," he said quietly. "Keep your cool. There's no room in this witch hunt for hysterics."

Then he practically flung my raincoat on my lap. We were nearing Union Square, and the street was flanked by buildings full of promises. I couldn't for the life of me remember what they promised, but I did have that feeling—promises about education and love and flowers and tomorrow.

Before I had absorbed what he had said, he was gone. The car lurched to a boggling stop, and he disappeared among the other tall well-dressed men that walked purposefully away from that block of promises.

I was still looking for Rick when the car passed. It was a dark-blue Ford, and from the driver's seat a man was peering at me. I had seen him before, against the flowers of the stall at Ghirardelli Square, with his feet planted like the sphinx on stones instead of sand.

That glimpse of the man's bland, searching face had a curious effect on me. It turned me to stone as surely as if he had been Medusa herself. I sat like a terrified, docile child as the car passed Union Square and the little row of shops and then ground to a halt at the turn-around.

As if from a great distance I heard a voice repeating itself, louder and with growing irritation.

"End of the line," it repeated with the vexation of long martyrdom. "End of the line, Miss. Turn-around. Everybody off the cars, please."

I stared at the cable-car operator who was leaning over me, his voice overloud in my ear. His Afro was immaculate, the white of his eyes clear and startlingly beautiful against his rich dark skin. Meeting my eyes, his role slipped for just that minute, and he became whoever he really was, instead of the man who ran the cable car as if it was his separate and inviolate empire.

"Are you okay, Miss?" he asked, his voice low now, and a little rough with concern.

I touched his hand, maybe just to know that we were both alive and human and all right. Then I nodded and rose to my feet. "I'm fine now, thanks," I told him quietly. "Thanks a lot. I'm fine."

I fled back up the street to the St. Francis.

Even before I started in the swinging door, I knew with a painful certainty that someone was in there waiting for me.

"Now who's paranoid?" I asked myself sarcastically.

I forced myself not to look at the lines of people in the lobby, not to fix my gaze on a man busily studying a tray of jewels at the counter. Only as I turned to step into the elevator did I really glance back. His back was to me, and he was on the mezzanine level, where the bar and luncheon place was. He was small and slender and middle-aged. I saw the fat mounds of the Japanese waitress's hair as she nodded to him in conversation and the squareness of the obi against her slender back. I knew without seeing his face that he was

89

the man who had followed me all weekend, the man at the flower stall at Ghirardelli Square, the man with the inconspicuous face staring up at me through the blurring windows of a stupid blue car.

I was indeed being followed by that wallpaper-faced man. And the only person I had to help me was paranoid and obnoxious, and I didn't even know his last name.

9

THE COMMITMENT

I had used up my dinner hour with that encounter with Rick. I repaired my makeup and changed my coat and fled back downstairs to get a cab. I couldn't disappoint Miss Tru by being late again this evening.

As the cab started south I saw those inevitable headlights following at that discreet distance.

"Go to hell," I whispered to myself, locking my jaws with anger. "Follow me to kingdom come. Sit outside the hospital and get paid by the minute. Follow me back and sit and play with straws in the bar forever. But when I find Mathew Martin, you're the one that's in trouble, not me."

Miss Tru's face showed the strain of pain that night. In an effort to distract her, I regaled her with every wild, gay adventure I could think of that had befallen Grand and me on our travels. By the time I left, her cheeks were flushed, and she was relaxed again.

"That's what it is all about," I told myself silently as I kissed her good night. "Her being happy is what it's all about, and Mathew Martin is way down the list on the priorities right now."

There is something infinitely soothing about a mechanical world that is running well. Encapsulated within the controlled humming of the elevator's rise, I felt myself relax slowly from my anger at being followed everywhere I went. I was even waxing philosophic about elevators, about how, since they lack both blood and judgment, they are free of the torments of anything but electrical failure, and therefore are small havens of peace.

Then my haven reached its floor, and its doors opened with the elegance of fine engineering, and I was thrown back into the world of men and their conflicts.

With wordless ferocity two men were battling in the hushed darkness of the hall outside my room. I flattened myself against the wall by the elevator in recoil from the brutality of their struggle. Like primitive animals at bay, half-crouching, they circled watchfully, then attacked and struggled. Rick's opponent wore something sheer and tight over his face, giving him an anonymous, terrifying look as he aimed a cruel blow to Rick's midriff, bending Rick over into a semicircle of pain.

Rick, suddenly recovering, caught the man's head in an arm lock, and the dull thud of their exchanged blows made me faintly nauseated. I wanted to cry out, to help Rick somehow, but the nearly silent scene was closed to me, to everything but their separate desperation.

In spite of Rick's agility, the big man slipped from his grasp and, circling, struggled something from a pocket. As he darted towards Rick I could see the quick glint of metal in his upraised hand, and I suddenly became unstuck from my wall.

I aimed a hard-booted kick to the knee joint of his right leg, and he staggered, momentarily off balance, the knife glinting at Rick's eye level as his arm flew up for balance. Rick caught his jaw with a crunching blow that sent his head backwards. For a frozen moment in time the man seemed to hold the posture of a flung puppet, arms outstretched and body curved almost gracefully in a backwards arch. Then he crumpled untidily on the floor, and I watched a pool of blood begin to seep through his mask from his smashed jaw.

Rick was beside me instantly, his clothes awry and the redness of abrasion beginning to stain his face. Before I could react at all, he was past me with his thumb on the down button of the elevator. He glanced back warily at the man on the carpet who showed no signs of ever rising, much less preventing our escape.

"We need to fade," Rick said tersely. "While you're uncovered."

A middle-aged couple was in the elevator. They stared at Rick with combined revulsion and curiosity as they huddled together in their mutual corner. Rick unconcernedly wiped the blood from his hand and stared back at the woman boldly. Maybe it was hysteria but I wanted to giggle. From her hairstyle I would put them from somewhere east of Salt Lake City, but not far. I could imagine her recital of this horrifying scene, the disheveled man with blood on his hands and in his eye and the grinning simpleton of a girl . . . and them alone in the elevator in the middle of the night in a strange city!

Never have two people left an elevator with more agility than they did when we reached the lobby floor. Rick and I wasted little time either. We shot through the lobby and onto the street, with Rick cradling my arm with his as if his hands were too sore to use in even a small gallant gesture.

"The parking lot," he nodded with his head, steering me towards the corner.

"Was that the man?" I asked. "Was he the one that was following me? He looked too big."

Rick mumbled something, "God knows who he was." His voice was tight with anger. "I just went up to wait for you to get home. He was already there trying to jimmy your door. It seemed easier to put him away myself than try to get the hotel dicks in time."

A look of pain crossed his face as we started for the garage elevator.

"You really hurt your hands," I said with concern. "I'm so sorry."

"I hope you can drive," he said. "I may have been guilty of overkill on that concrete jaw of his. Incidentally, where did you ever learn to kick like that?"

"Soccer," I explained blandly. "He was a much easier target than a ball."

Rick gingerly fished his keys from a back pocket and handed to me. I unlocked his little red sports car, and he crawled in to turn his hands in the light from the dash and examine them warily. Tentatively he clenched his fists and then loosened them with a wince.

"We need to get some hot and cold water and something antiseptic," I decided aloud, studying the wounds.

"I'll live," he grinned. "Thanks for the concern."

"Thanks for the defense," I said. "Was he really breaking into my room?"

"No doubt about it," he said firmly. "Any idea what he was after?"

"The crown jewels," I suggested. "We little country girls from Indiana are great on baubles."

"Anything in there about Martin?" he asked quietly, that same expression of confused rage that I had noticed earlier.

"Not a thing," I said, then realized what he meant. "You really think this whole business is tied up with him? What has he done? Why are they after him?"

"Later," he said resignedly. "Let's hit the road. We need to talk."

As I eased the car into the traffic of Union Square, I glanced at him. "Any special direction?"

He was frowning thoughtfully. "Just stay on this street," he said after a minute. "I'm trying to think of some place we can rap."

"You must have a place," I suggested.

He grinned at me oddly. "Not that I could take you to."

"You do need to do something about your hands," I said. "Hey, do you know Sausalito?"

He frowned at me. "I can find the Trident on a foggy night, why?"

I shoved my purse across to him. "There's an envelope in there. I have the keys to a house out there. Maybe we could fix your hands up and 'rap' at the same time."

I'd forgotten the condition of his hands. I watched him struggle with the purse. Then I pulled over on a residential street and opened the envelope. He was flushed with embarrassment. "Talk about the useful male animal," he groaned, flexing his swollen fingers.

Miss Tru's sealed envelope was a neat package. It held two keys on a ring and the small folded note I had watched her write. There was another note giving me what seemed explicit directions on reaching her house in Sausalito. The quickly scribbled note was the one that gave me the second of pause. It was scratchily written with haste but was clearly a warning. "There is something fishy about Mel. Stay away from her." It was signed with a large T for Tru.

95

"What's up?" Rick asked, watching my expression.

I shook my head. "Just a funny note from my injured friend."

"You're not laughing," he accused me.

"It's not that kind of funny," I admitted, pulling the car back into traffic to start north again.

The fog that had buried the city cleared as we crossed the bridge. The headlands loomed giant and dark and crenelated against the fog bank beyond. I drove in silence trying not to remember the scene back there in the hotel hall, trying to erase the sickening sound of Rick's fist against the man's face and the funny crumpled way he had fallen on the rug of the hall.

Following Miss Tru's scrawled directions, I left Bridgeway and took a road up into the hills above town. Sausalito was a semicircle of gaiety hugging the curve of the bay. In among the trees, the lights lessened as we rose and the distant howl of dogs replaced traffic sounds. Even the fog horns were muffled, and there was only the hum of the car's motor as it labored up the incline and the faint cry of night birds in the thickets that lined the roads.

"You really act as if you know where you are going," Rick commented as I made the turnoff into the woods.

"It's an act I have developed," I told him. "It seldom convinces me, but it sure fools strangers."

I slowed down to let a lumbering raccoon have the right of way. He stopped in the middle of the road and turned to stare blindly into our headlights before loping awkwardly off into the brush. The road dead-ended at a curve of the wooded hill. A driveway wound upward to disappear into blackness, but the mailbox at the base of the drive was marked "T. Lyons" in letters that reflected the lights from the car.

I eased the little car up the curving drive and into a carport beside a seventyish Chevrolet that was littered with leaves and whose blue color was clouded with dust.

I set the brake carefully, and Rick and I sat a quiet moment in the car listening to the lonely call of a night bird and the scrape of wind-harried leaves against the roof of the carport.

"What an eagle's nest," he commented after a minute.

"Wait until you meet the eagle," I told him, getting out. "She's my favorite old bird in the world."

"You say she's sick somewhere?" he asked.

"You might say so," I explained bitterly, fitting one of the keys into the kitchen-door lock. I flicked on the light inside the door, and a huge, rambling, untidy kitchen sprang into view. It was a warm yellow room with houseplants on the sills of the windows and a stack of magazines on the corner desk. The room looked like someone had just stepped out. A pot of coffee sat in its grounds, and a tray of brandy snifters sat unwashed on the counter top. But the plants in the windowsill were limp with drouth, and as I pulled my finger across the round breakfast table, a dark line appeared in the layered dust.

"Someone broke in here," I explained, "hit her on her head and fractured her skull, broke her collar bone, and almost killed her." I rinsed out a copper teakettle and set it to boil after a few trial-and-error runs with the knobs on the stove.

"Did they get the guy?" Rick asked sceptically.

"They're following leads," I said acidly. "She damned near died, the burglar tried to set the house on fire, and they have 'leads'."

I must have sounded bitter, for he shrugged and turned away from my glance.

"It's not a pretty world, Clem," he reminded me almost apologetically.

97

After I dusted the round table I sat him there and went to look for medical supplies. The house seemed to go on forever. Beyond the formal dining room was a huge sunken living room, with book cases almost to the ceiling on the wall facing the fireplace. The burned drapes had apparently been removed, but smoke stains on the wall and deep burned scars on the carpet along that wall reminded me of the failed arson attempt that had been Miss Tru's salvation. An easel stood at an angle along the long windows that faced the view. Pots of paint and a stained smock completed the look of someone's having just stepped out . . . several layers of dust ago.

Beside the master bedroom, which was again lined with books, I found a bathroom with a well-stocked medicine closet. A pervasive scent of mildew came from the towels strewn about on the tile floor.

"You'd never make it as a medic," Rick informed me when I had finished dressing and bandaging his hands. "I could star as the Son of the Mummy."

"So it's antiseptic . . . feel any better?"

"Marvelously better, thanks," he said.

"I know there's a drink here for you somewhere, but I couldn't guess where," I admitted, pouring the coffee into the filter pot, which I had had to wash out before I could use.

"Coffee is fine, Clem," he said seriously. "I'm guilt-struck now. I really need to talk. To confess."

With the mug in both his bandaged hands, he sank into a deep chair that sat by the open fireplace.

"You are really Mathew Martin," I said.

"You wouldn't know it if I wasn't, would you," he queried.

I shook my head. "You don't fit the descriptions. But . . ."

He held the steaming brew to his face and then pulled it back, cradling the cup carefully. He looked funny and handsome and kiddish all at once. Then he raised his eyes to me, and that essence of his sadness struck me again, making me gentle somehow.

I leaned forward.

"Confess."

He grimaced and rose to come over and join me on the divan.

"Look, Clem," he said seriously. "I went over this whole thing in my mind after I met you at Ghirardelli today. I thought about it all evening while I waited for you to get through gadding around and come back to your hotel room. I'm not saying I wholly trust you, but I'm short of choices. I made up my mind to level with you and try to get you to do the same with me. We obviously want the same thing . . . to find Mathew Martin."

I stared at him, pulling away a little, "You don't mean . . ." I began threateningly.

He laid his white paw on my arm. "I mean I lied to you. I mean that I haven't the vaguest idea where Martin is. Not the vaguest!"

"Oh, you . . ." I was helpless with anger. This fraud . . . this paranoid, hopeless liar!

He didn't pay any attention to my interruption. His voice went on calmly and seriously. "I don't know what your reasons are for finding Mathew Martin, but I'm worried as hell about him and I'd join forces with the devil if I thought he could help me find Martin."

I looked at him. He had led me on to believe he was in contact with Mathew Martin; he had bullied me and beaten off an intruder for me, and I didn't even know his name. The wind stirred beyond the long windows and the trailing strands of the eucalyptus swayed, stirring the lights of the view beyond the windows. It was cold and still and far. No one in the world knew where I was or with whom. I should have been afraid. Instead I felt cool and removed and very objective. I guess a kind of shock had come over me after that unbelievable day.

"You make it sound so urgent," I said slowly. "It's not quite that way with me. I don't have to find him tomorrow. I could even forget the whole thing. I don't have to be followed around by hoods, lied to by you, have my room broken into. I can just get on a plane and go back to Indiana and let that package rot in the bank vault. I just came to pay Mathew Martin a debt that is due him, not get myself scared to death."

"Okay," he said, rising and walking disconsolately to the window. "If that is true, then if I were you, I would take the next limo to the airport and check out of the whole thing." As he stood there against the view, the broadness of his back shut out most of the lights so that he seemed larger than life somehow, shining in silhouette like a man blazing with some unearthly light. Then he laughed shortly. "I'm here for the same kind of reason. Only mine is an older debt. I owe Martin something no bank vault could hold. I think he's in trouble, deep trouble, and I owe him enough to work at getting him out of it alive."

"A different kind of vault?" I asked hesitantly.

He shrugged and turned to me. "It's almost a cliché, Clem. It *is* a cliché. There have been a dozen grade-B movies built around it, and they are still running them when a big football game has the other channels tied up."

"So if it's worth saying a million times, I can afford to listen one more time," I suggested.

"Mathew Martin saved my life," he said bluntly. "He saved it when he didn't have reason to, with considerable danger to himself, and when no one would have ever known if he had decided not to."

"That's a debt," I conceded slowly into his silence.

"Now he's in trouble," he went on tersely. "He's in trouble and is fleeing for his life. I know that like I know my name."

"But what has he done? Who is after him?" I asked.

He shrugged. "It's the big holes in the puzzle that are giving me trouble. All I am working on is that because of Mathew Martin I wasn't deep-sixed. And nobody is going to scrub him out without my doing all I can to keep it from happening."

"When did this all happen—this danger to him?"

Rick ran his fingers through his hair with an abstracted air. "Maybe when he was born. You can't imagine this guy, Clem. He's the greatest in the world . . . when he's great; and he's the bitterest, sickest guy in the universe when he turns on himself."

"I don't get that 'on himself' bit," I admitted.

"He's got this fixation," he said slowly. "He's a guy with no name, no family, no history of his own. He calls himself a doomed man. That's what he says, right out, Clem. 'I'm poison,' he says. 'Everything I touch, I kill.' He's been beaten and running since he was a kid. Guilt stalks him like a hunter. All he's ever known how to do is run."

"And that's what he's doing now, running?" I asked.

Rick sat down by me on the divan, crossing his long legs and staring at the floor beyond. "A different way somehow," he seemed to grope for words.

Suddenly my head was full of voices. Like a Greek chorus, they rose and fell and spoke and answered each other, not meaning anything particular by themselves, but by their harmony and counterbalance seeming to rise into a rhythm of portent.

My grandfather's voice, slow and measured. "A debt, a secret debt."

The fierce harshness of the old man at Corners West, "No son of mine."

The woman in the darkness of the fog-ridden night. "He was gone just like that . . . no word to anyone."

And strangely, Mel's voice turning suddenly brittle in the cool brilliance of the San Francisco darkness, "I remember nothing. . . . There was no one before Bran."

The baleful melody of those shadow sounds moved my mind towards something dark and ugly that my grandfather would have called a premonition.

"You've gone away, Clem," Rick accused me suddenly. "You've gone clear away and left me here."

I turned to him. "It was only for that minute," I promised. "I was getting ready to listen. I'd like to hear it all, Rick, clear from the beginning. But I had to be ready."

He looked at me warily. "Okay, Clem. I'll give it to you. You can help me with it when I'm through, or you can take off clean. It'll be your baby. But are you sure you're ready?"

"I'm ready," I told him quietly and was suddenly terribly, terribly afraid.

10

THE EAGLE'S NEST

Dawn leaked over the Sierra, spilled into the wide wine valley, and finally rose in colored layers over Berkeley. We had
talked and listened and hungered and eaten until the night
was a verbal confusion that spun in both our heads. Miss
Tru's cupboards had yielded the inevitable quick foods that
are the refuge of the lone, but we were past complaining that
the great bowls of hot chowder were reminiscent of tin and
the saltines had seen a crisper day. The last pot of coffee
was a muddy memory in chill mugs when Rick finally fell
silent and looked at me. His eyelids were heavied with fatigue, and a stubble of darkness stained his face. Then he
grinned—a strange out-of-time grin that seemed to be an
expression remembered from another, purer era . . . maybe
when he was ten and didn't know how to use a razor, and

violence was something you experienced vicariously in a theater seat at Saturday afternoon movies.

He reached for my hand with his white bandaged paw and said, "When this is all over, Clem, remind me to get to know you. My instinct tells me there might be somebody there I'd like."

"Then you must have an instinctive weakness for limp-necked women," I grinned back. "I'm a good five hours past holding my own head up."

"I'd offer you a shoulder, but I think our lives are complicated enough," he admitted.

"Truer words . . ." I sighed.

"Are we any closer?" he asked dubiously.

"Only if your pieces and my pieces can somehow be matched together," I admitted.

He rose tiredly and stretched like a careful dog. "I'll take my leave. I'm not even going to offer you a ride back to the hotel. You're better off here. Pile into bed and call your old eagle whenever you waken. But think on it, Clem. The missing piece in this puzzle is the rope that will hang Mathew Martin if we don't find it."

I walked to the door of the carport with Rick as he left. He stared into the night thoughtfully as he sat in his car. Then he leaned against the steering wheel and looked up at me.

"Look, Clem. If we can get you moved out here without your bird dog sniffling along, it will be all to the good. When you go back to town to visit your friend, stop by the hotel, pack your things, and tell the manager that a messenger will pick them up after five. That way you won't tip off any watchers that you are clearing out."

"Okay," I nodded docilely.

"Not going to accuse me of being paranoid?" he grinned up at me.

"I guess I'm infected now too," I admitted.

I watched from the doorway as he backed the car carefully down the steep drive and then listened to the roar of his acceleration as he took off down the mountain towards civilization. A medley of birds fluted morning from among the giant trees, and the smell of cough drops hung in the air. I pulled a slender twisted leaf from the tree that overhung the carport and crushed it between my fingers as I went back inside. This was the smell that had filled my room at the hotel, this was Celeste of the sniffles, this was the eucalyptus that banked the drive to Miss Tru's house.

In the torpor of my fatigue it seemed to me that all those things that were evoked by the medicinal astringency of eucalyptus oil were mysteriously joined. The elusive and forever fugitive Mathew Martin, the loneliness of my growing up in strange rooms with strange people, and Miss Tru propped in a hospital bed, all were somehow joined and interwoven. I laughed softly to myself. This is the real heritage of living with a Greek scholar. You forget that things can fall accidentally into place; from some subconscious cluttered corner of your mind comes a suspicion that all of life is a vast design planned and executed by somebody on Olympus.

Whether the Gods or sheer whimsey were operating, I was still too full of the night behind me to follow Rick's instructions.

I rummaged in the closets and made myself at home.

Miss Tru's taste ran to capacious high-necked gowns with bibs of heavy woven lace. After letting the shower beat me with blazing water, I curled up in one of her gowns and pulled a granny afghan over my knees to supervise the arrival of the new day.

Something in me was reluctant to lie on that freshly

stripped bed where Miss Tru had so nearly been murdered.

Vietnam. I had to sort through the pieces of Rick's story for myself. Rick is that kind of guy who seems to put a lot of verbal weight on trivia and hit the important things with a lighthearted slap.

Rick's voice had brought me a series of sharp unforgettable images that were all interwoven with Mathew Martin.

Four years in Vietnam with Mathew Martin. Patrols and jungle fighting and villagers with round-eyed children strapped to their rickety backs.

Mathew Martin, the man who never even turned up for mail call, who played silent chess with himself as adversary, who was a quiet listener but never a talker. A man who was universally accepted as the perpetual stranger.

I mused on how their unequal friendship had begun.

"We were on patrol together," Rick had said quietly. "Nasty wet weather with nothing firm underfoot and the trees dripping with fetid moisture and always the need for silence because of Charlie.

"Matt was like a cat in the jungle, silent-footed and with eyes everywhere. I'll never know how he was warned, but the warning came a split second too late. Martin caught me across the shoulder and knocked me down flat into the mush of a slimy bog and was there beside me instantly. I heard the bullet as something separate from myself, but the sting of it was real—and mine. He half dragged, half carried me for fifty yards or more, staying behind trees and deep in the brush before we could stop to stanch the blood. I was sick as a kid, not from pain but from nausea and not being able to breathe.

"Somehow he got me back to a medic and help. Except for hassling nurses, my war was over, but I had lived it out because of Martin."

I found it was hard even to imagine Rick that way, weak and helpless and inarticulate.

"We had almost served our time when it happened. Martin used to come see me, taught me to play chess in a halfhearted way, as if he knew I didn't have that kind of strategic mind. And I talked to him."

"Didn't he ever talk to you?" I had interrupted. "You always mention your talking and his silence."

"Not talk really. But a guy gives himself away even in silence," Rick had mused aloud. "And I had a lot of time to try to piece him together."

"There was family, for instance. After thirty-five years of making it, my own family blew it up back home. There were these letters, careful, explanatory, civilized, and between and among the lines vituperative. My mother and dad had seemed welded together forever in my mind. And my sister Stephanie was caught in the cross fire. She couldn't take sides because, like me, she was close to both of them. Her letters were wails of anguish. There was only one thing she wanted—escape—so I worried about her aloud."

"And Mathew Martin listened?" I asked.

Rick nodded. "She left college, and with the money I sent her went to New York where she got a job. It isn't much. She is just a cog in a typing pool, but she is alone, out of the divorce ugliness, and trying to think herself into who she is. She's happy now, describes her little place and the things she picks up to furnish it. She is planning to enroll at City College in New York later and work toward something better.

"Martin used to listen patiently to all of this. 'I'm no expert on the family bit,' he once said laconically. 'A bastard kid who's pushed into the first open slot isn't troubled by allegiances.'"

"But they must have cared a little to take you on," Rick had recalled countering him.

"The money came every month," Mathew had said in reply. Rick remembered that Mathew had made a move as he spoke, moving in his queen for a proximity check covered by two rooks. "The woman had some heart but no spine; for the old man it was the check he never realized I knew about."

Rick had wandered on, reminiscing.

One time when Mathew Martin was visiting Rick, there was a lot of scuttlebut about a fragging charge that had been brought against an enlisted man. Nobody had doubted the soldier's guilt but Mathew Martin.

Rick had argued with Martin about the case. "The soldier had provocation enough," he pointed out, "and circumstances are pretty damning. Motive, opportunity, and a grenade—how much more evidence do you want?"

"Every hole in the wall is not a window," Mathew had said angrily.

When Rick was telling me about the incident, he described Martin's reaction as coldly furious. Then he added that Martin had seemed apologetic about his outburst.

"He didn't really apologize, Clem," Rick had said. "It was more as if he was trying to explain his own involvement."

I tried to remember exactly the words he had quoted from the "explanation" of Mathew Martin, but they came back to me only as flat skeletons of sentences. That must have been the way Martin had said them, for Rick had spoken them flatly without elaboration.

"I was a kid once," Martin had said. "There was something I wanted very much. One man stood between me and what I wanted. The man was killed and I was there when it happened. I had it all . . . as you say—the motive, the opportunity, and the power. But I was also innocent with no way to prove it."

"And they nailed you?" Rick had asked him, knowing that those bare bones of the story were all he would ever hear from Martin himself.

"No way," Martin had told him. "I took off running, and I haven't slowed down since."

Whatever happened between the lines of that bare recital had to have been in the summer of 1959, because that was when Martin had disappeared.

I told Rick about the Martin couple out at Corners West and my separate encounters with them. "He left there thirteen years ago," I added. "That's a long time to keep running."

"Martin mustered out while I was still having the operations on my chest," Rick explained. "Before he left for stateside he came by to see me for that last time."

"Anything I can do for you under the bright lights?" he asked before he left.

"I gave him the standard sex patter about The Condor and Broadway and all that, but he broke in on me.

"Later, Rick," Mathew said. "Later we'll play the grown-up-boy games. I have something to do first. Then we'll get around to living."

"Anything special in mind?" Rick had asked him.

"Nothing I can spill now," Martin had replied. "But when I settle, I'll get my address to you. I'd like to see you again." He had grinned a funny way that seemed to mean a lot to Rick. "Aren't many guys I ever say that to."

Rick had fallen silent.

"So he left?" I prodded.

Rick had nodded. "He left and came back, and I didn't hear anything for a month or more. Then a card came. It had a San Francisco address. 'Feel free to use the facilities,' was all it said and was signed with the double *M* that Martin always used."

By the time Rick was released from surgery and flown home and discharged it was March. When he got to San Francisco, he went straight for the address that Mathew had sent. The landlady told Rick that Martin was gone, and there was no forwarding address. She did say she'd take his name and number, just in case.

Three days later Mathew called. They got together and spent a long evening pubbing down the peninsula.

Rick asked him about their getting a place together, but Martin shook his head. "I'm on a project," he explained. "It isn't anything you want to get mixed up in. When it's over and I'm clean, then I'll look you up. Leave your address with the old landlady—she's secure."

"He didn't explain this project or why it was dangerous?" I had asked.

"A clam," Rick said with a frustrated look. "But I got the feeling that it had something to do with that old score he wanted to settle. I got the feeling that he was tired of running and was trying to clean it up for good."

The last segment of the last leg of the night's fire fell with a crumpled thud in Miss Tru's fireplace. I stared at its shower of sparks with that sick premonition heavy in my chest, remembering Rick's voice falling into a lower key, his mind forcing him back to his last encounter with Mathew Martin.

"I saw Mat just a few weeks later, only by chance. I caught him on the street, Clem, and he almost threw me off when I caught his arm. His eyes looked strange and wild, and kind of haunted."

"Stay away, Rick," he said in a low warning voice. "Don't be seen near me, and don't ever speak about me."

"I protested that maybe I could help, and he shook his

head. 'I made a misstep,' he said bitterly. 'Now I'm the hunted. You don't want to be caught in the cross fire.'

"I've been looking ever since, Clem," Rick told me bitterly. "I leave word with the landlady and nothing happens. This sense of tension keeps rising. That's why I rose to the bait of your ad. Something is ready to blow on Martin, Clem, and I need to help."

"He couldn't be blowing this all out of size?" I asked. ". . . a lonely guy like that with an old score to settle?"

Rick mused. "I thought of that. But then when I saw those tails on you at the Square and caught the guy at your door—" he paused, "I might as well level. That fight at the door of your room shook the hell out of me, Clem. With that mask I couldn't tell a damn thing, but in build and condition that man with the jimmy locks could have been Mathew."

I leaned forward and stared at him.

"Do you think? . . ."

"I don't know what to think. But you're from that idiot town where this all began, Mathew's town, and we sure didn't imagine those private eyes on your tail."

I rose, trailing Miss Tru's nightie along the rug, and went to the window that overlooked the slope of the house. I stared down at the banks of oleander, marguerites, and the ground cover of ice plant that clung to the slope beneath the giant eucalyptus trees.

Suddenly I realized that someone was there. A man was working in the garden below. His back was to me, and he seemed tall and abnormally slender in that foreshortened view. My mind was too much on the mystery of Mathew Martin. I watched the gardener turn with an armload of cuttings and toss them towards a pile gathering at the base of the garden. As he turned I could see him better—dark, gleaming hair to the shoulder surrounding an anonymous bearded face above an open-throated work shirt. This would be Miss Tru's friend.

Another morning I would call to him, I promised myself, and ask him in for coffee. Now I was brain-bent. I turned from the window and curled up on the divan with a blanket, falling almost instantly into a deep and troubled sleep. I was plagued by one of those strange dreams where you know all the time you are dreaming, and yet you cannot force yourself awake. It was a dream of running. Sometimes I was running myself, always in the dark, down long twisting roads and helpless to cry out. I did not know what pursued me or what I was pursuing. That was the difficulty. For someone else was running too. The steady frenzy of those running steps echoed and reechoed in my mind, sometimes ahead of me and sometimes following. Always there was the exhaustion of my own terror and my wordless screams bursting forth silently from aching lungs.

11

NAMELESS SILENCE

The early afternoon sun angled through the window of Miss Tru's hospital room, striping her coverlet with light and giving her frailness an ethereal quality. I had jested to Rick about her being an old eagle—she looked much more vulnerable than that propped against pillows with a lacy jacket over the stiffness of her regulation hospital gown. Her head was bent over her open journal. She wrote slowly, seeming to savor the letters forming from her pen. Her hand holding the pen resembled a kind of lace claw, a webbing of bone and blue vein barely netted to usefulness by thin spare skin.

As she lifted her head at an angle to recall a phrase, she saw me in the doorway. The journal closed with a sharp snap as she turned to me.

"Finally dragged yourself from the arms of Morpheus,

eh?" she asked with a wicked grin. "Or am I naming the wrong man?"

"You are an evil-minded old lady," I rebuked her, bending down to brush her forehead with a kiss.

"In politer society it is called experience," she came back tartly. "When I called earlier they told me you hadn't been down nor answered your bell, so I *presumed* you were asleep."

"You were presumptuous indeed," I laughed, tossing my raincoat over a chair to sit down. "I just never went home at all last night. How's that for a maidenly confession?"

"Very San Francisco," she said dubiously. "I always knew you were a fast learner, but that wasn't what I had in mind. Did you go home with Mel and Bran?"

"No," I shook my head. "I threaded my way through the fog and the lights of Bridgeway, up the rocky crags and around the raccoons . . . ."

"You went to my place," she broke in with delight. "Is everything all right? How did you like it? Good girl!"

"I adored it," I admitted. "Slept in your bed, burned your fire logs, ate your soup, and ogled your gardener. I even drove your balky beast over here without benefit of navigator."

"Funny thing," she mused. "I came out here because nothing was left in Prathersville but my dead hopes. I told myself that if I stayed near Mel, the closest I've ever had to a child, I would be making a good move. It was a good move, but for different reasons. Mel and I are not close . . . have never been since Ambrose died, and she walled herself off that funny way. But the freedom of my life, that nest in the trees . . . it's been the greatest."

"An aerie," I replied, remembering what Rick had said.

"My aerie. It's been fantastic."

"You're not afraid up there?" she asked. "After what happened to me and all?"

114

"Love it," I assured her. "Didn't see a solitary soul but your gardener hacking away at the bulging green."

She frowned as if puzzled, then smiled. "That would be my friend Troll. Good boy. It's good knowing that he'll keep the garden in shape till I get back."

"Troll?" I laughed. "There aren't many bridges he could fit under."

"Oh, that's not his real name. It's a joke between us. He calls me Witch and I call him Troll, and we both leave it at that."

"I think he won a little on the exchange," I told her, "but that's for you two to dicker over. Say, what was the enigmatic little note about Mel?"

She wriggled uncomfortably and the sides of her mouth turned down. A pettishness entered her voice. "I don't know about that girl. Last night she was so strange and hexy somehow that I just had the instinct to warn you away. She is a moody one."

"Her husband covers for her beautifully."

"If he even notices it," Miss Tru snorted crossly. "What she needs is a good swat instead of all that tender acceptance. But she'll never get it from Bran. If love was ever blind, he has the classic disability. He called me this morning, spent a good half hour on the phone literally pumping me about you. I guess she's never mentioned you to him, which is at least strange since you were the only *close* friend she ever had in her life."

"She said something funny to me last night, after dinner," I admitted. "She said that Prathersville didn't exist for her, that she had no past before Bran."

Miss Tru sighed angrily. "That's a stupid pose. As if you could wipe out time with a wave of a wand. We all have things and times we would rather forget, but they're there . . . and all the self-hypnosis in the world won't erase them."

She paused and stared speculatively out the window. "That's funny that she should say that. I guess it's all wound up with her father's death. That was when she changed, and that must be what she is running away from."

Running. The word brought back my dream of the night just past. I shook my head to try to erase the wild memories of that dream. But I could hear the haunted running feet of that dream even there in that sterile hospital room. Footsteps, my own and others, echoing along the devious pathways of that threatening darkness.

"It's unnatural it is for a girl to mourn her father that way," she went on quietly. "But it does explain why Bran knows nothing about you."

I grinned, "There's not all that much to know."

"He was insistent," she said, "almost professionally interrogative—your age, your father . . . he knew you were Sylvia's child."

"Then he knew my mother?"

"Everyone knew your mother, Chryseis," she said flatly. "She was the most beautiful, most sought-after girl that ever broke hearts all over Indiana. He went to school with her, you know, before she went away."

"He's that old!" I cried with astonishment.

She nodded. "Sure is holding up, isn't he?" Then she shrugged. "But then why shouldn't he? He lives in a dream world. He worships perfection and has managed to make his world look that way. He's rich, he's socially prominent, he's married to the girl he always wanted . . . 'the perfect woman,' he calls her, though I think she's a self-centered little hysteric."

"When you love someone you are supposed to see them as they really honestly are," I quoted my grandfather.

She stared at me; then her thin hands picked idly at the striped white coverlet of the bed.

116

"I sometimes wonder if there *is* a Mel, Chryseis," she said quetly. "I have seen her as so many people—an inhibited little prig with her mother, growing up; a wild, strange, fey creature when the two of you were together. Maybe I'm cross at her now because I'm disappointed." She smiled a strange way. "Before I left here for Jackson's funeral, things were different. She was happy. She had flowered somehow, with a glow of happiness that rode on her like a sheen. You can't imagine how great it was, Chryseis. Then I came back and that veil had fallen again. She doesn't even eat. Oh, damn. Why am I wasting our valuable time clucking like an old mother hen?

"And besides that," she wrenched a little in the constriction of her cast, "any minute now that cursed bell is going to clang and a bunch of liver-faced nonentities will be squeaking around here on their rubber shoes doing *things* to me."

I grinned at her. "Get well quick. Come home, and I'll clomp around in Danish clogs and cook you indigestible things, and we'll read together."

"Did you and Jackson read together?" she asked quietly.

I nodded. "All my life—and even more those last few years whenever I came home from school."

"I can guess what he asked for," she mused. "The special nine lyric poets of that period he loved?"

"From Alcman through Pindar," I nodded.

" 'But the greatest of them was Pindar,' " she said sternly, and we both laughed. That was always the final phrase that my grandfather said when we talked of "his poets" or read their lines.

The familiar thin bell sounded in the hall, and a scrape of chairs signaled the departure of those few other visitors that I had seen along the hall.

I rose and shrugged into my coat. "Isn't there something I can bring you, really, Miss Tru?" I asked.

She grinned crookedly. " 'The best of healers is good cheer' —just to show off my Pindar. But don't make the trip clear out here again tonight. Mel phoned twice after Bran's call, and they'll probably be after you for the evening. Just have fun in my house . . . and be careful on those hills."

"Will do," I agreed. I left meekly under the baleful disapproval of a white-clad woman waiting with ill-concealed impatience outside the door.

Maybe it is because of all those years of tight school discipline, maybe I just naturally have a weak character, for whatever reason, I have this awful tendency to slip from reality into my own fantasy world the minute the screws are off. Nothing was better, nothing was changed, Mathew Martin was still an elusive fugitive, but something about the way the wind swept a salty tang in from the sea and the cocky march of the houses up and down the San Francisco hills made me giddy with pleasure on the ride back to town. I rolled down all the windows on Miss Tru's car and drove through the city at the top speed limit, letting the wind whip back my hair and beat my face until my cheeks felt cold and as red as winter apples.

I was almost to the bridge when it registered on me what Miss Tru had said about Mel's calling twice. Mel would be trying to reach me at the hotel. For some vague reason I couldn't have explained, I didn't want Mel and Bran to know I had moved on out to Sausalito yet. My California geography was vague, but wherever they lived in Marin might seem too close for comfort, yet . . .

At a phone booth in a shopping center, I got Mel's number from the operator.

Mel's voice was different, almost soft with relief. "Gosh, I'm glad you called, Chrys," she said. "I've been trying to get in touch with you all day."

"I slept in," I explained, "then went out to see Miss Tru."

"She's all right, I guess?" she said hastily.

"Fine."

"Where are you now?"

"Just leaving the hospital," I lied.

"Let me see," she was silent a minute. "How about if I meet you somewhere at your hotel? We wouldn't have much time but I'd love to chat."

"Marvelous," I said. "How long would it take you?"

"Only twenty minutes," she said, "give or take five. At the Dutch Room?"

"That's four-thirty under the windmills," I concurred, relieved that it hadn't been a dinner invitation that I would have had to weasel out of.

I was on my second cup of coffee when she arrived. I watched her stand in the door and look about for me, she looked very small and frail in street clothes, the collar of her immaculately tailored dark coat just touching the curve of her hair. As she crossed to me I was startled to realize that her walk was a little too careful, as if she were having trouble with unsteadiness of her legs.

"She is beautiful," I decided, "unnecessarily beautiful." She shrugged out of her coat and chattered at me about the traffic on the bridge and a dozen other things at once. I guess I wasn't listening to her words, only to some frantic pressure that seemed to push them from behind, so that they came out awkwardly and tripping and without any timing at all. I felt suddenly cool and distant and wary, as if she were threatening me with her friendliness.

Her immaculate makeup covered a flawless skin, and under a slim line of blue, her eyes—typical Scorpio eyes I remember having decided when we were all wrapped up in astrology—were darkly veiled under carefully stiffened lashes.

119

I felt very troubled and gauche, as if the wind of my drive had swept away any pretense of sophistication that I could have possibly mustered.

"You're awfully quiet," she said suddenly.

"I was admiring you," I admitted frankly. "You're a stunner."

She frowned crossly. "Oh, don't say that. You sound like Bran." Then her lip caught in a gesture of remorse. "That was ugly of me. I'm sorry."

I shook my head. "You are, that's all."

She smiled, dismissing the comment, and reached across the table to lay a perfectly manicured hand on my sleeve. A large marquise-cut diamond glinted in the light as she moved.

"I wanted to talk to you, Chrys," she said unhappily. "But this is an impossible place. Let's ride somewhere . . . I'll take you in my car. I'll show you my favorite place, and we can really talk."

The sharp staccato of her sentences betrayed an almost impossible nervous tension. I was so tempted to blurt out to her that she should say what she had to say and get it over with, but I guess I was intimidated by her distress. I rose docilely, and we crossed to the parking garage where she whipped into a sweet little silver Jaguar XKE that somehow fitted her like a second identity.

Somehow in the moving security of the car, we both relaxed. For one thing she didn't have to meet my eyes. She watched the traffic and guided the responsive little car in and out of traffic and onto the bridge.

Her face was flushed now, and she chattered constantly as she drove.

"This is a special place we're going. You can see every boat that leaves San Francisco from here. It's a high place . . . you know what I mean?"

Her eyes searched mine a moment and I nodded. A high

120

place, a special place of escape. Our retreat in the old summer house . . . that was the old Mel.

"I wanted to talk to you, Chrys," she said quietly. "I don't know what got into me last night. I know I was boorish."

"Not at all," I protested.

"I haven't told you properly how really sorry I am about your grandfather. I've thought about him so much just lately . . ." her voice trailed off. "Do you remember that picture of his? The one that used to scare me? The one with the white birds?"

I nodded as she rattled on. "This place has birds like that. They always remind me of that picture—the way they wheel and circle or fly overhead in great angles of moving light."

For that few minutes she was Mel again, the intimate air of confidence, the evoking of the old times. I began to relax and was completely off guard until I noticed her covert glance at the clock set in the dash of her car.

There was something she had come to do or say, and her time was running out.

"You are getting paranoid from Rick," I told myself sternly, but I waited warily as she turned off the highway and made a turn or two that started the car up towards the headlands and the sea.

"There is something I feel bad about, Chrys," she said softly. "I told you a lie last night without meaning to. You asked me something and I told you that there was no Prathersville for me . . . that I didn't remember. I do remember, but . . ." she grimaced. "This is hard to say without sounding disloyal to Bran . . . but Bran is very possessive . . . very jealous. I know he doesn't *seem* that way, so open and charming, but he is really a green-eyed monster inside about me. He can't bear to think of any life for me before the one we shared. Do you understand that?"

"It's not very realistic," I said warily.

"He isn't very realistic about a lot of things," she agreed. "I just make it a policy not ever to talk about anything before . . . and that solves it."

"I felt a little shut out," I told her. "It was as if you had wiped me out too, along with the Prathersville square and the First Baptist Church."

She laughed softly and touched my hand. "Not you, Chrys, not our times. Other times." Her voice stopped, and she caught herself almost visibly.

"Then I should never mention the old times around Bran? Is that what you wanted to tell me?"

She looked at me squarely, then nodded. "That's right," she said. "Especially other names, other people."

Mathew Martin's name lay betwen us unspoken for a full minute. I was the one that broke. Being me, I escaped into levity and let the minute to put that question pass forever.

"The curse of a coven of witches on he who bothers Bran," I said ostentatiously.

She giggled, actually giggled.

"And their fingers will turn to newts and their princes back to frogs," she finished. "Did you ever find out what a newt was?" she asked guilelessly when our laughter stopped. "I used to think of all that stuff we said, and I didn't understand the half of it."

"And I still don't," she went on, "but it makes me have horripilations when I think of the spells we put on people."

"When I last saw them, they were in good health," I assured her. "Even your cousin Horace!"

Mel swung the car into a small parking area; beyond it a ragged fence bore the legend "State Park Area." Down the path that led through the gate I could see a huddle of weather-grayed buildings that looked desolate . . . not buildings really, I decided, more like abandoned embattlements from some forgotten war.

She didn't stir from behind the wheel. She stared off into the blue sky and at the points of the Golden Gate Bridge that rose above the hill we were facing. Then she laughed.

Her laughter was quick and natural. She spread her hands flat on the steering wheel, and her eyes assumed a dreamy, whimsical look that I well remembered.

"How good it was then, Chrys. And that's not all that long ago!" She caught herself as if she had been indiscreet. "But it's wonderful here, it really is. And after things settle down with Aunt Tru, I get to show you all my things. The woods . . . you'll love the redwoods in the morning, Chrys, early, before the fog clears so it weaves ribbons in among their heads like shrouded giants.

"We'll have tea in the Japanese Garden at Golden Gate, and there's a garden there that is only for smelling. It is intended for blind people, but it is fabulous to walk there in silence and be clothed by sweet scents.

"But this is my knoll," she stared past me almost dreamily. "It's here that I always remember your grandfather's cranes. Bran first brought me here because we could watch the ships carrying his produce to sea. Even the city is a polished toy place from here. And always the white gulls riding on the wind. Like your grandfather's cranes."

She caught herself sharply. "Now, see what I've done. I've sat here chattering and used up almost all our time. I have to be home and long-skirted and serene for Bran when he comes. But we can catch a minute's view, can't we?"

She leaped from her side of the car, and I followed her swift footsteps past the embattlements I had seen from the car, past a great hollowed area that appeared to be the shells of living quarters, and then an armament storage area. Finally we scrambled up the thickets on the slopes to the high point.

She stood silent for a moment as we looked down on the

bridge and the city and the beach far below. It was almost a communing. I huddled in my raincoat trying to keep from being blown backwards by the wind that steadily pressed against us.

A fleet of small fishing boats was coming in. They swung a wide arc to avoid the center current of the bridge and with their white fans of wake moved in a measured row around the curve beneath us. "That is Kirby Cove," she finally said, pointing down. "People camp there and things. The big one on out is called Bonita." Her voice trailed off and she caught my arm. "Back, back, always one must go back."

She dropped me at the hotel within minutes.

"It was fun, Mel," I said as I got out of her car back on Union Square. "Thanks so much."

She looked almost startled and then said, "It *was* fun, wasn't it?" as if that had been the furthest thing from her mind.

After giving her a decent interval to get across the bridge ahead of me, I started towards Miss Tru's house. I thought of Miss Tru's wistful irritation. "I have seen her as so many people." Miss Tru was indeed an acute old bird. And I wasn't sure that I liked the clever, polished, ingenious Mel of this afternoon at all.

I had filled the trunk of Miss Tru's Chevy with groceries before I wound up the hill road towards home. Rick's car was already parked in the carport. The top of the car was down, and my luggage bulged from the back seat.

Since Rick was nowhere to be seen and the door was locked, I walked around the deck to where the stairs led down to the steep lower garden. Rick was at the bottom of the steps staring off into the garden. At the sound of my arrival, he looked up without smiling and started up the steps thoughtfully.

"Ants in your ice plant?" I asked.

"Funny you should ask," he said quietly. "Is there any reason why anyone would want to do in your old eagle?"

"Miss Tru?" I asked. "Absolutely not. She is the world's most harmless species."

He helped me unload groceries and then my things. Only a faint bluish tinge on his left cheekbone betrayed his tangle with my caller at the hotel. His eyes were clear and blue and troubled as he stared at me.

"Clem," he said quietly, "call me paranoid all you want, but while I waited for you I tried to break into this place without smashing a window—just to check out that burglar story. There's *no* way. Whoever tried to do her in had a key to this place."

Through the open door behind me I could hear the pip of gulls passing over the wooded hill from the bay to the sea. The scent of eucalyptus clung to Rick's clothes and filled my head. There was a darkness in the air as I stared at him without speaking. What kind of a world was it where an eccentric old lady was beaten nearly to death by someone she trusted?

"I want to believe she left something unlocked," I told myself fiercely. "I don't want to be seduced into seeing a threat in every turn of an hour." But my grandfather's voice, reading at twilight in a lonely rom, echoed in my head. I could see my needle patiently going in and out of a needlepoint sampler as he spoke.

"Slowly but surely withal moveth the might of the Gods."

PART THREE

Shadows on the Opposite Wall

Human beings . . . like ourselves . . .
see only their own shadows, or the
shadows of one another, which the fire
throws on the opposite wall of the cave.

PLATO

12

WAITING

A collage of silvery lichen was massed on the oak logs that Rick heaped into the fireplace. I slumped down on a low stool to watch the fire start, a slow crackling protest that gradually rose into curling fingers of flame. I stared numbly, sorting things in my mind, trying to absorb Rick's discovery that Miss Tru's assault had been something more personal than the mindless invasion of a common criminal.

Rick went away and then returned, handing me a steaming mug of coffee. "Ten minutes 'till pizza," he announced proudly.

"You're kidding," I said with a start.

He grinned at me sideways. "I looked at your groceries and decided you had more ambition than practicality. There's nothing there that either of us could make a meal of."

"A roast," I protested, "vegetables . . . fruit . . ."

"I stopped on the way for pizza," he broke in gently. "In ten minutes it will be hot enough . . . okay?"

"Okay," I grinned. "I guess I kind of worked off a list like Vinnie used to send me with."

"Whatever a Vinnie is, it doesn't start on supper at twilight," he announced mildly, letting himself down on the rug near me. "I don't guess I need ask why you're in the blue funk."

"Miss Tru," I said slowly. "Who among her friends would have a reason for killing Miss Tru?"

"We can start way before that," he said drily, "and work up. What was that long-ago crime that Mathew was framed for? A guy doesn't survive four years of jungle hell and come back to stir up trouble unless it was *big* trouble."

"You lost me somewhere in there," I said.

"I'm being paranoid again. I have this sick gut belief that the attempt on your old friend is tied up somehow with Mathew Martin . . . not that he did it, but that they are somehow linked . . . just like the tails on you and the guy at your hotel room."

"Do you have anything to back that up?" I stared at him. "Anything at all?"

"I don't," he admitted, dropping his eyes from mine. "I only know that something in my memory of Mathew Martin, something in his own conviction of his being doomed, infected me. I keep feeling that you and the old lady have gotten caught in this curse he carries around like pawns in a very morbid game."

"But it's so farfetched," I protested.

"Not so much," he pointed out. "Everything seems to lead back to that town. I know towns like that. I grew up in one of them. Mine happened to be in New England, but the stage is the same: interbred families, ancient hates, old secrets, and the ugly webbing of the past undermining all of the present."

I shivered. "And Mathew and Miss Tru are both from there. But she didn't know him."

"Have you asked her?"

I shook my head, "No." I hesitated a long moment. "It never even occurred to me. Isn't that strange."

"Maybe not," he reassured me. "After all, you said it was a secret search—that would have stopped your questions."

"No," I reflected. "I never even thought of it. But I will. I will ask her about it. There were always people she knew—her 'funny friends' as Mel called them. People no one else knew, tradesmen and farmers and . . . just odd people that were her friends. The old Japanese gardener whose family sold vegetables on the square on Friday afternoon and Saturdays. She even went to visit him when she was back for Grand's funeral. She knew people no one else knew."

"Mathew qualifies for that," he said drily. "And as for this Mel . . . she's from there too, the old eagle's niece?"

I nodded.

"And did she know Martin?"

"She did," I confided suddenly. "She lied when I asked her, but she did. According to gossip she and Mathew had a kind of puppy-love thing going a long time ago." My voice trailed off, and I could suddenly feel something dark and ugly form in the back of my mind. Mel.

"And Mel's married?" he asked. "Where's he from?"

"Prathersville," I replied glumly.

"The Bay area is really Prathersville west," he said hopping to his feet. "Come, give me a hand cutting pizza." He slapped me on the back. "I don't mind cooking our meals, but I do balk at doing the whole thing alone."

After we ate the last crumb of the pizza by the fire, Rick grudgingly admitted that I had done a good job of buying fruits and nuts in the shell which we fed into the fire, starting small private conflagrations in among the embers.

I tried to explain Prathersville and Mel and Bran to Rick, but he kept coming back with strange questions that I had never managed to put into such a nice straight line.

If my grandfather and I were so close, why was I always sent away? Was there something about Prathersville he was shielding me from?

If Mel and I were the best of friends, why was I not a part of her wedding, or at least told of it before it was a fait accompli and Mel was gone with her husband halfway across a continent?

And finally, if Bran was the big-wheel agronomist that he was, why did I keep remarking that he was such a dreamer? "A scientist and a dreamer?" Rick almost hooted. "The very terms are antithetical."

"I barely know the man," I admitted. "That one evening, that's all I've ever seen of him."

"You never ran into him socially in that tight little town?"

"Never once," I admitted. "He's just a lot older. Old enough to be my father in fact."

"And Mel's?" he asked.

"And Mel's," I agreed unhappily—that ugly shadow of half-formed thought was pressing against my mind again.

"That happens," he said quietly, pitching a handful of almond shells on the embers so that a shower of sparks rose. They turned to pale scarlet and finally burst into flames. "There are supposed to be only three roles that woman chooses men for . . . lovers, fathers, and sons. Maybe she needed the father she lost."

"That's ridiculous," I almost shouted.

He looked at me levelly. "Is it?"

I wavered, then fell silent. "What brothers me is the

word 'role' I guess, I wouldn't want to be loved for an image, a role. I'd like to think I was loved for myself."

"We all would," Rick admitted, "but we don't usually get that break. After all this time I have finally accepted what happened to my parents as natural and inevitable. They married at nineteen, they were teen-age lovers and never managed to see each other as anything else but aging teen-agers. They fought like kids and made up like kids and provoked each other with an immaturity they never showed in other circumstances. In the end, they failed each other as adults because they couldn't see each other as the persons they really were. The things that each of them needed— wisdom, understanding, and just to be accepted for them-selves—they had to find somewhere else."

"I've just decided never to grow up," I said flatly.

"Join the Peter Pan Club," he laughed. "Just don't kid yourself that you're the first one that tried it. And be pre-pared for a helluva jolt when you take off flying." He rose and stretched and grinned at me. "I need to get back home for some sleep." He pulled me to my feet beside him. "Do you want some last-minute advice before takeoff?"

I nodded, standing there by Rick in the flickering light. This was a great guy. That was my debt to Mathew Martin. Without the search I would never have met Rick Sanders, and that would have been a loss.

Something in my look at him caught him off guard. He looked at me strangely, then turned away.

"Get on that hospital staff," he said tersely, hassling his coat out of the closet and onto his broad shoulders. "Get the old eagle released. Promise them a nurse, a hospital bed— promise them a sterilized room if they ask it—but get her home where you can watch over her. Just in case. . . ."

Rick and I had just stepped out into the carport when the roar of a motor broke the silence of our little street. Mel's

Jaguar pulled in behind Miss Tru's car with an authoritative snarl.

Bran was driving. He grinned eagerly at me as he hopped out of the car. "Noisy little beast, isn't it?" He glanced at Rick, puzzled and said, "Oh, hi," before circling the car to open the door for Mel.

They had obviously been to a party. Mel was immaculate in deep wine red with ropes of mingled pearl and garnets wreathing her throat above a deep décolletage. She looked stunning, and as secret as a shadow.

The world's most awkward moment hung there in the carport before I recovered. Rick and I, rumpled from floor sitting and sleepy from fire and pizza, stared at them like something extraterrestrial.

"Well, hi you two," I finally discovered my voice.

Bran was apologetic. "We are not interrupting anything? You weren't on your way out."

"On the contrary," I said swiftly. "I'd like you to meet my friend Rick Sanders."

"Sanders?" Bran said questioningly. Then his hand shot forward to meet Rick's hand, and all his instant ebullience was there, the forty million watts of instant charm bathing Rick with brilliance.

Mel had only nodded. She was pale, suddenly deathly pale. She shivered and pulled her dark fur wrap around her shoulders and laid her hand intimately on Bran's arm.

"I'm *sure* we're interrupting Chrys and her friend," she said quietly. "And anyway, it's late."

I should have justified the expensive training in social graces that had been bullied into me for all those years. I should have urged them inside, offered drinks all around, and done the civilized hostess bit. Instead something in me froze in the already chill air of the carport. My moment of silence was quite communicative, I guess.

"You're right, Mel," Bran said, patting her hand. "We tried to get you at the hotel, and they said you'd checked out. Then Auntie told us where you were. We really just flew by to see that you were here and settled in all right."

"Thanks so much, Bran," I said. "That was very nice of you. And I am fine."

"Sanders . . ." Bran repeated thoughtfully. "I didn't realize that Chrys had other friends around here to watch over her. Are you local or from another time and place?" He asked the question lightly, as if in jest.

"Neither," Rick said calmly. "We met through a mutual friend."

I didn't want to look at Mel because of the tense hollowness of her eyes. What I really wanted to do was blurt it out . . . just like that . . . "a mutual friend named Mathew Martin." But I didn't have the courage or gall to do it.

I think it was right there, that minute in the carport, that I decided for sure and certain that Mel had been more than lying about Mathew Martin. Miss Tru's talk about Mel's glorious spring—had that been Mathew again. The thought made me a little sick at my stomach, and I reached for Rick, blindly, without looking.

All of a sudden my head ached . . . a slow steady beating that began somewhere like a clock ticking inside, like the slow measured movement of a metronome on the polished surface of a piano. Mel's face had started time in my head . . . a time that was being measured, a time that was running out.

Rick knew something was wrong. He slid his arm under my elbow and supported it gently.

"We'll meet again, I'm sure," Rick said lightly. "After Miss Lyons comes home."

"They are going to let her go?" Bran asked brightly. "That's good news. She'll be happier here at home."

135

I nodded automatically to the ticking in my head.

I practically leaned against Rick as Bran backed the car expertly down the drive and took off in a grinding of gears. Then Rick turned me by the shoulders and looked into my face.

There, under the hooded lamp of the carport, he stared at me a long minute.

"Want to tell me about it?" he asked gently.

I shook my head. "It's wild," I stammered, "wild and ugly, and I'm scared."

Wordlessly he drew me close. I just leaned against his solidity there in the cool night. Off somewhere a dog howled, a slow aching lonely cry to the moonless night. Slowly Rick's body warmed me. When he pulled away, he pressed his lips softly to my hair.

"Okay, Clem," he said gently. "Tuck in bed. And remember, time is always with the one who waits well."

I was glad to have things to do during the waiting. I wakened to find my head full of plans about getting Miss Tru home. Rick was right. She had to come home where I could watch over her.

I was starting out to the car with my purse full of lists, when I heard the scrape of someone in the garden. I went to the deck and looked down.

"Hey, Troll," I called.

He straightened and stared up at me, obviously startled.

"I'm bringing Miss Tru home right away," I told him. Then I grinned. "Your Witch."

"Great," he said earnestly, squinting at me in the early light. "Then she's getting along all right?"

"Sparky as ever," I told him. "You'll have to come have coffee with us when I get her settled in."

He saluted with the battered hat that covered his shoulder-length hair. "My pleasure."

There wasn't any problem getting Miss Tru released from the hospital. The director was affable going on eager at the prospect of her leaving the premises.

"They know a good out when they see it," Miss Tru grinned wryly. "I haven't won any personality contests here. A tart tongue draweth few flies."

"You didn't want flies on your tongue anyway," I reminded her.

"How long will it be?" she asked me for the third time. "All of a sudden twenty minutes sounds like forever."

"You miss your aerie," I laughed.

"And my privacy, and my friends," she added. "Have you seen Troll again?"

"This morning early," I told her. "I told him you were coming home right away. He does pick some strange hours to get ecological!"

"He's a strange man," she said contentedly, as if it were the most enviable of appellations. "Did I ever tell you how we met?"

As I listened, the scene was as graphic as if I had been there. Miss Tru was caught with a flat tire on an out-of-the-way road and was struggling to work a jack with lively epithets.

"I was almost at a bridge when the thing went," she explained. "He came walking out of the shadows of that bridge as if he had grown out of its timbers . . . this big tall guy in half-service half-civvies and grinning from ear to ear."

"I asked him what he thought was so damned funny," she went on. "I had a bruised finger in my mouth and was a little short of laughs."

" 'Your language made me homesick for the army,' " he

told me. Then he pushed me aside, and that malformed travesty of a jack worked for him like a charm."

"We talked while he worked. I kidded him about being the first good troll I'd ever found under a bridge.

"I watched him while he got the tire fixed, and it kept growing on me that he wasn't a stranger really, that I knew him from somewhere, some time.

"When he finally straightened up and grinned at me, I knew I was right. 'You aren't from around here, are you?' I asked. Something slid in his face kind of, something wary. 'I'm from nowhere,' he said flatly, 'Strictly from nowhere.'

"'Join the club,' I told him. 'I'm from nowhere too.' Then I asked if I could give him a lift.

"'I wasn't going anywhere,' he admitted, 'just prowling around looking.'

"I happened to have been on my way to the top of the headlands above Kirby Cove. Bran and his export business had gotten me interested in shipping schedules. I told him I was going up to watch a tanker go out, and he was welcome to come along.

"We had a good three hours together," Miss Tru grinned that funny crooked grin that I remember from when I was ten. "We prowled around the old artillery emplacements, those strange hollow quarters where fireplaces still mark abandoned walls, and watched a fishing fleet come in. We'd missed the tanker because of my flat. Then he came home with me and we had sandwiches and coffee and talked for another hour.

"He was fascinated by my garden, by plants he had never seen and the challenges of working on a slope like mine."

"Did you ever figure out who he was, or who you thought he was?" I asked curiously.

She smiled, that curious halfway-cynical smile that some-how evoked something wild and mystic from another time.

"We've all been so many people, Chryseis, at different times, in different places. Even if I thought I knew him in one of his lives, it is the now that our friendship lives in, and both of us live with it comfortably."

"So he comes for coffee and friendship and prowls in your ice plant," I said. "And you never call him anything but Troll?"

"Why should I?" she retorted sharply. "Anybody who says 'Good morning, Witch' at the top of his lungs in my garden deserves no better!"

"I'll buy that," I giggled.

"He seemed pretty pleased to hear that you were going to be back home good as new." I paused thoughtfully. "Do you suppose that place you took Troll is the same old fort that Mel drove me to yesterday afternoon?"

"Without a doubt," Miss Tru nodded. "It's her favorite place. She goes there a lot. In fact, it worries me sometimes— it's not the safest place in the world."

"There was nobody up there yesterday when we went," I countered.

"I'm not concerned about anyone else hurting Mel," she said enigmatically.

"The world doesn't seem to hurt people like Mel, they do it themselves. Part of her died too young, in that accident at the mill when Ambrose died, leaving her with only a sniveling mother and no sense of long truth," she sighed. "She didn't have a Jackson Maxwell in her life, Chryseis. You and I know that whatever you want to call the mountain, Olympian clouds swirl about the heads of its Gods, that what men call coincidence or fate or kismet are the same old machinations by another name. By committing herself to forgetfulness Mel abandoned the wisdom of thousands of years.

"But something within her searches for that continuity, so

139

she goes," she sighed. "She goes and stares at the endless line of the sea and the crashing surf below and grieves."

"It's a beautiful place," I said softly, hoping to distract her. "And later, I'll take you there again."

She smiled. "I go there a lot now . . . I am not a forgetter."

I was all over Marin County and San Francisco that next few days. I rented a hospital bed and all the other junk that was needed for Miss Tru's care until the final cast was off. I inventoried the cupboards and kicked myself and Vinnie and fate in general that I had never learned my way around a kitchen properly.

During one of my frequent visits to Miss Tru I managed to slip in a small inquisition about the night of her injury. Rick's attempt to enter the house without keys haunted me, but I didn't want to tip Miss Tru to our ugly suspicions about the attack coming from someone whom she trusted.

"I don't understand how anyone got into that place without breaking glass or anything," I commented in a puzzled way. "It seems tight as can be to me. Are you sure it was thoroughly locked up?"

"Of course it was," she said almost angrily. "I'd have to be senile to stay in a secluded place like that without being careful about locks and bolts."

"Now don't take off on an attack," I kidded her. "I just wanted to hear more about how it happened. Was there anything special about that evening? Had you seen anything, heard anything?"

She snorted angrily. "I'd seen more and heard more than I wanted to, that was for sure, but it didn't keep me from locking the house up after Bran and Mel left."

"They'd been there that night?" I asked.

"You might say so," she said bluntly. "They'd had dinner at the Mandarin and stopped by on the way home for a cognac with me. I made coffee, and we had a fire and it started out like any other evening . . ." her voice trailed off and she frowned. She lifted a hand to her head in a tentative puzzled way, then sighed. "One thing about cracking your head real good . . . things leak out."

"Then I gather the rest of the evening didn't go just as usual?" I prodded.

She shook her head. "It got ugly. I don't even remember now how it started." Then she grinned and fished in the drawer for the journal. I watched as she leafed swiftly back through the book and then paused.

As she read the entry, her frown deepened and she sighed. Then she snapped the book shut with a sharp slap.

"I started it," she admitted. "Mel was stiff and withdrawn that way she gets, and Bran and I talked while she sat there like something marble off the cover of *Vogue*. I asked her a question, and she didn't answer me—didn't even seem to hear me. It was as if she had gone somewhere leaving her body empty in that chair.

"It really got to me. I told her I thought she was losing her marbles if she couldn't keep her mind on a single social conversation.

" 'Mel's under a strain,' Bran said, or something like that. It always irks me when Bran tries to explain my own blood niece to me. My God, I changed that girl's diapers. I know her better than he will if they were married a thousand years.

" 'Don't you wish it was that simple?' I asked him caustically. I never have been long on tact you know, and cognac is no help to tongue control. I've discovered.

"Then for no reason Mel burst into tears and flew off to the bathroom.

"Bran started making excuses the way he does and it got

to me," she admitted. "When he gets mealymouthed like that, my gorge always rises a little anyway, and I was in no mood for it. I reminded him that she had been mine a long time before she was his, and I knew some Mels that maybe he didn't even dream about.

"He made the mistake of scoffing at me, and I really got riled. Something I only half remembered and still need to check on came back to me, something about the fire. I blurted right out to him that I remembered Mel when she had been in love before, and she wasn't any walking zombie then—she was all light and life and happiness.

"He got mad—mad and cold and ugly, Chryseis. I was amazed because I never thought there was that much fire in him.

"He challenged me on what I meant by that, and I told him right out that I had always had suspicions about that fire. It almost looked like providence to me that Ambrose died when he did, because he sure as hell wouldn't have let Melanie marry a man old enough to be her father if he had lived.

"He was on his feet in an instant and paced back and forth with cold fury. He called me a meddling old fool and said I better keep my mouth off his marriage. No telling what else he would have said, but Mel came back then, her mascara still staining around her eyes and her face as white as a sheet. They went home, cold and formal and quickly."

"I can't believe you didn't tell him off for that meddling remark," I commented. "After all, you are her only relative around here."

She ducked her head in a funny way and didn't meet my eyes. "Maybe I have meddled, Chryseis," she said slowly. "In fact, I know I have, and I ought to have character enough to be sorry for it. But I never thought it would end this way."

142

I was still puzzling that enigmatic remark when she raised her eyes to me again. "You were gone, Chryseis, when Mel was in love that once before. I've seen her happy, and it's something you can't believe. I'm selfish enough to do most anything to bring that shine back to her eyes. But you never know when you start something . . ." she trailed off again.

The conversation wasn't making any real sense to me anymore. I wanted to ask her then if she knew Mathew Martin, if he had been the boy of Mel's first love; but Miss Tru was too agitated. Her bony fingers picked at the coverlet in a kind of frenzy and I backed off. I started telling her about Rick, anything to distract her from what were obviously memories too stressful to leave her with.

"He's a big red-headed Scotsman," I told her. "He hangs around a lot and is really a marvelous guy. He's going to come out and see that you get moved properly."

She squinted at me narrowly. "Seems like you got something going awful fast for a beginner."

"Think on Plato," I said severely. "You need a little practice with pure thoughts." I scraped my chair hard as I took an airy good-bye.

"Tomorrow," I said. "Eat your last professionally prepared meals with gusto, for tomorrow morning you have to come home and be fed by a rank amateur."

"I defy you to despoil good groceries worse than they do here," she replied acidly, not heeding the fact that a nurse was standing in the door to suggest I was overstaying my leave.

I ducked my head apologetically at the grim sentinel as I passed. Miss Tru's voice followed me into the hall. "I got a gift bottle of wine today, Chrys," she called. "I'm saving it. It was from somebody named Rick!"

Rick. I grinned. What a great guy! I'd only mentioned it

in passing, but he'd fixed it up for me. Then my mind flew back to the dozens of small errands I had to complete before meeting him for dinner. We were going to celebrate by dining out at Ondine's my last night before taking over the full-time job of nursing, and guarding, Miss Tru.

13

THE RETURN

The city was brilliant with morning. The ferry from Sausalito trailed a lace fan wake between the bridge and Alcatraz. Morning still stained the east bay with color, and a single small sailing craft was making a graceful way through Raccoon Straits. The day could not stay that lovely. Already beyond Point Bonita we could see the gray mass of fog moving inward towards the bay. But as we crossed the bridge every swaying gull was brilliant with the sun that glittered on the city and the bay.

It was Rick's idea that he take me out to the hospital in his car so that I could accompany Miss Tru home in the ambulance.

"I feel guilty as hell," I confessed as I slipped in beside him that morning. "I've shot two weeks of your life with my problems, and we're no closer to Mathew Martin than we were when I got here."

He shot me an oblique glance as he eased into the traffic starting across the bridge. "Possibly, but possibly not," he said thoughtfully. "Remember, my visceral fantasy about all roads leading to Prathersville."

I giggled. "Any visceral problems you have today are probably linked to béarnaise sauce and soufflé Grand Marnier."

He groaned. "They do know how to whip in a calorie or two, don't they?"

"Fabulous," I said sincerely. "And thank you again for a great evening."

I glanced seaward from the bridge, straining my eyes to see how fast the fog bank was moving. The great stirring cloud was vibrant with color, a deep gray along the sea line, with a hint of rose as its roundness swirled upward.

"Some day it will be clear enough for you to see the Farallones from here," Rick told me. "Afterwards, we'll take the boat trip out. I'm a little hung up on sea lions, and I like them best in their own places."

Afterwards. I wished I could get time to straighten things out in my mind. I wished I could lose that stubborn sense I had of time beating away steadily towards an end. I wished I could even project what that end would be. My dark growing suspicions of Mel, my insidious way of adding two and two and two and getting not six but twelve were getting to me. The end of all this was too hidden and obscure for me even to search with my mind.

We were greeted with open arms by the entire staff on duty on the second floor. Rick grinned wickedly at me as a skittering nurse hastened us along to room twenty-three.

I don't know how I ever restrained a wild giggle. Miss

146

Tru, looking as if she had been up for hours and had another good day or so riding with her, was implanted on a stretcher as if it were an angled throne. She seemed to fill the whole of the room with the strength of her personality alone. In carefully categorized groups about her were her possessions. A cluster of ruffled magenta cyclamen nestled with spidery white chrysanthemums. On the other side a small overnight bag stood beside a paper bag that bulged prominently.

She clutched a large dark purse to her side and, from under it peeked the mottled cover of her Journal. Her lipstick was a little askew, and her hair leaped from her scalp as if in astonishment. She was one old eagle ready to fly, and no doubt about it.

She cocked her head at Rick in the doorway, studying him with the piercing blueness of her eyes. Then she snorted. "So you're the Scot. And you even look able to manage that little baggage."

"It isn't always easy," he confessed with a grin, lifting her hand gallantly.

A thoroughly intimidated male nurse jiggled her stretcher nervously from behind.

"Stop that fluttering," she barked crossly. "You're making me seasick."

With a nod, Rick took control of the stretcher from the relieved man. Smoothly he started it towards the elevator. We made a triumphal exit down the hall past the open doors whose occupants had temporarily at least discarded apathy for the headier joys of curiosity.

When Miss Tru was safely stowed into the ambulance and Rick stepped out, her face fell.

"You're not leaving me to the mercy of these scoundrels," she said.

Rick laughed. "Only temporarily," he assured her. "Haven't you heard, I practically live at your house."

She cackled. "Don't tell me you are bringing me home to chaperone you two big overgrown kids."

"It's no fun misbehaving when there's nobody to disapprove," he told her grinning.

"I'll be out a little after five, Clem," he told me. "Just in case you need some help starting dinner."

I made a face at him as the ambulance door swung shut. Miss Tru cackled.

"Where did you say you picked up that great creature?"

"Ghirardelli Square," I answered honestly enough.

"What is that he calls you?" she asked, angling her head to stare after Rick.

"Clem," I said disgustedly. "It makes me sound like a redheaded rube strummer in a barn-dance group."

She laughed heartily. "It does lack the classical tone," she agreed.

Miss Tru fell silent as the ambulance started over the bridge. She turned her head on the stretcher so that her eyes moved gently and naturally over the shapes of the bay, like a hand caressing a familiar and cherished shape. The crescent curve of the city into its bay, the stark vertical mass of Alcatraz and beyond, the steaming staggered busyness of the east bay.

Angel Island and Belvedere seemed only a reach of the hand away in the brilliant light as the ambulance left the Bridgeway to begin its slow tortuous climb to the house in the woods. The fog bank that had been forming away out at sea was creeping slowly over the headlands threatening an end to the blaze of sunlight.

By some miracle we beat the fog to the house. Miss Tru was silent and watchful as the ambulance attendants transferred her to the hospital bed I had had installed in her

148

room. She looked about the room slowly, at the freshly filled sherry bottle on her bedside table, at the mass of marquerites spilling from the great black Indian bowl on her dresser, and then at the window which was open so that the fresh scent of her garden stirred the drapes against the wall.

She retreated, as my grandfather always did in times of stress, to familiar and borrowed words. Her voice had lost its usual harshness as she spoke.

"I know how men in exile dream of home, Chryseis. Thank you for all this."

"Thank *you*," I told her brusquely. "You must realize how much it means to me to be needed and wanted."

Quickly I unpacked the little overnight bag that Mel had taken her in the hospital so I could go prepare her lunch. Her eyes were heavy with exhaustion, and I felt that a few quiet moments alone would restore her strength. The paper sack was filled with miscellany . . . a few magazines, a paperback book or two, and some soiled linen. In along the side was the bottle of wine from Rick. I admired the label. It was Cabernet Sauvignon by Mondavi.

"That's for tonight," she said happily. "Your Rick promised he'd be back, and we'll use it for toasting. I still don't know how you did it."

My mind was already halfway to the kitchen planning the lunch I meant to serve her. I didn't really know what she meant by that remark. It could have referred to any one of a number of things. Maybe she meant she didn't know how I had managed to connect with a great guy like Rick; maybe it was the sheer happy fact of getting her home. It didn't seem to matter. She was happy, and I went off humming towards the kitchen to preheat the oven and get the casserole in on time.

She napped a little and then browsed among the huge stack of accumulated magazines until I had lunch finished.

We ate on trays in her bedroom. Just as I filled her second cup of tea the fog made it all the way to the windows, walling off the glass and muting the sounds of the fog horns that had begun to pulse shortly after we got home.

It was a dark fog, and the wind that bore it whipped streamers of the giant eucalyptus tree against the house. I wished that the wind would cease, or at least that the tapping of the leaves would quit matching the steady drumming of the countdown that still ticked in the back of my brain.

"It is over," I told myself sternly. "It is over and she is safe." I would be here all the time; Rick would bring us anything we needed; she need never be alone for even a second. *Nothing* was going to happen. But still the leaves tapped their steady rhythmic beat like a clock that would one moment run down.

Miss Tru ate a good lunch, then slept most of the afternoon, dozing with her head turned towards the fog-draped windows. Her hands were so white and slender that they rested like transparent leaves on the whiteness of the turned-back sheet.

After I had done all the preparations I could think of, I lit the fire and curled up to knit, trying to concentrate on anything but the problems that must be faced now that Miss Tru was home. Mathew Martin was as far from found as ever, no matter what Rick said, and there was my added terrifying conviction that Mel was somehow the villain in the piece.

I do not share Miss Tru's indulgence towards disorder. My mind is like a terrier that shakes a thing until it either is destroyed or assumes some sensible shape. No amount of self-delusion could keep me from sorting the pieces of the puzzle and coming up with the terrifying suspicion that Mel was indeed mad, and possibly a murderer.

It made such hideous logical sense. Take the case that

Mathew Martin had indeed been her first love . . . ("I am a Scorpio," she had told me that long time ago very solemnly. "A Scorpio loves only once and forever").

Take the case that Mathew had been lost to her in the aftermath of her father's death, and in resignation or despair she married Bran. And Bran would have settled for that, I decided. His adoration was so complete and his character so ebullient that he would be the kind of a man who would believe that having a wife was the first step, and that teaching her to love could come later.

But let Mathew Martin come back all these years later. Let them meet and the love still exist. Miss Tru had talked about meddling, and her depression about how it had all ended. I shook my head. The way Mel was acting, she could indeed be "losing her marbles" as Miss Tru so vulgarly expressed it. And Mathew was gone. There had been Miss Tru's comment of how Mel had bloomed in the spring, that special way, and when she returned, Mathew was gone and Mel was sunk again into this morass of depression. Mel had the keys to this house, I know she must. And Mel could hardly have kept from hearing the inflammatory argument between Miss Tru and Bran.

A long time ago Rick had talked about pieces falling into place in this puzzle. They seemed to be interlocking now, but I didn't like the picture.

The meddling was still the missing key. Had Miss Tru broken up this reborn liaison between Mathew and Mel, presuming it existed; and if she did, who had entered that house to still her tongue? Was it Mathew? He would have reason enough, and it would certainly send him underground. But it was Mel who would have had the key.

Suddenly I couldn't stand living with my own thoughts.

I thrust my knitting aside and rose swiftly. I went to the door and looked in on Miss Tru. To my relief she had wakened and was writing in her journal with the strangest quizzical look on her face.

When she glanced up at me, she cocked her head pertly. "You haven't done enough, Chryseis," she said sternly. "I have thought of another job for you."

"At your service," I laughed, conscious of the embarrassed apology behind her dependence on me.

"You must have explored the house by now," she said. "You know the two rooms downstairs?"

I nodded. She wrestled a key from her ring and handed it to me.

"In the one on the right of the bottom of of the stairs, there is a locked closet. It is shelves." She lifted her journal. "There are three shelves of these books there. I want the one that would include the summer of 1959—the year my brother died. There's just something I want to reread. The dates are lettered on the back."

"And you're supposed to be the disorganized one," I kidded.

I took the key and started for the door just as the doorbell rang. She glanced at the clock on the dresser.

"Good Lord, it's time for our handsome caller. Don't bother about the book now. Let him in and we'll get it out later."

Rick stood in the doorway with a huge spray of roses, head down at his side as if he were embarrassed by their presence.

"I'm not going to let you in until you tell me which of us you came to see," I told him sternly.

With his free arm he hugged me lightly, so that rose petals scattered on the floor.

But he grinned evilly. "A man does like a house with a wide range of choices," he explained. "How's the old doll?"

"Slept all afternoon and is probably in there primping for you right now," I told him.

"It smells good in here," he approved.

"The roast," I explained. "And if it isn't delicious, it is the fault of Miss Tru's cookbook, not me."

"That's my Clem," he said solemnly. "Pass the buck. Want to put these in something?"

While I searched the upper cupboards for a tall vase I heard him hallooing at Miss Tru's door. "Make yourself decent, I'm coming in."

"Decent indeed," she shot back. "If I looked decent it would be under false pretenses."

I was carrying the vase through the hall when Rick came out of her room. "Put it there on the coffee table, Clem," he said. "She's agreed to let me carry her out here by the fire. Don't you think pillows on that divan would work?"

I shook my head at him. "I can see myself losing ground fast," I told him. "But what a great idea!"

Rick managed it all, piling and fluffing pillows and carrying Miss Tru like a child. From her spot on the divan she could command a twin view of the crackling fire and the mist-shrouded windows beyond.

"Now this is something," she said happily, looking from one of us to another.

Looking back, I try to remember the sequence of events of that evening—what we talked about, how the time passed, but it is all blurred in the shadows of the following hours. I know the windows darkened so that Miss Tru turned on a small lamp by her divan. I know I made a dozen trips to the kitchen to turn the small round potatoes browning in the roasting juices with slender carrots and little French beans. I know that Rick refilled the log basket and Miss Tru beat him at dominoes handily, and with shouts of glee, while I tore lettuce for the salad and listened grinning from the other room.

It must have been almost seven when she called to me, "Chryseis, the wine!"

"You'll find glasses above the refrigerator. I have a great announcement to make."

I had taken all those things in by the fire . . . the glasses and a towel for the wine and a strange silver wine opener that I found in a kitchen drawer. I had barely set them down when the phone rang.

It was Bran. "I'm still at the office downtown," he explained, "and about to start home. Mel and I have guests coming tonight so I thought I'd check and see if Auntie had gotten settled in all right."

"Couldn't be better, Bran," I told him happily. "We have her ensconced by the fire for a drink before dinner."

"Good show!" he said heartily. "Now I can buck that bridge traffic knowing the old bird is in her nest and happy again."

"You were sweet to call," I said. "My best to Mel."

"Another of your male admirers," I kidded Miss Tru, returning to the living room. "Brandon in his glass tower calling to check on your well-being."

"She may have to devote her convalescence to writing a book on how to attract young handsome males," Rick suggested modestly.

That scene is all clear to me. Miss Tru was pale, but her white hair was toned to pink by the light of the fire. The fire reflected on the freshly polished wine glasses, and Rick struggled with the cork of the bottle with determined strength.

Miss Tru filled our glasses a careful one third each, the Cabernet gleaming like blood against the light.

"By privilege of age and infirmity, I get to propose the

first toast," she said sternly. "But first I have an announcement to make."

"Hear. Hear," Rick shouted loudly.

"My God, you sound like something out of Lewis Carroll," she snorted, grinning. "I thought a lot about my house here when I was in that miserable hospital. And after you got here, Chryseis, I thought more. It's been a great place for me to live but it's always lacked something. Now I realize what it needed. Houses have to be shared with something. The past is good enough, but this poor stack of nails and sidings has neither a past nor a future with only one old baggage owning it. Mel has always disliked the place, thought it was lonely and somber hanging here in the fog half the time. So I just gave it a future. Chryseis, you are now half owner of this bear's nest. And I could tell the difference this afternoon when you brought me home. The place is happier, it's warmer and realler. All by means of a small legal document.

"I have just spent the best day ever in this house, staring through its windows, hearing Chryseis off somewhere banging and humming to herself the way her mother used to when she was a child.

"Do you remember Jean Patou, Chryseis? Rick, he was an old French blackguard who used to help me with my garden back in Prathersville. He shambled around in an antique black truck and bib overalls and a black felt beret."

I nodded, grinning. Jean was one of the local characters that every child knew. The hum of his mower on Grand's yard had wakened me many a holiday morning when the sun was barely up.

"He was one of those high-handed liars who would spin a whopper when the truth would work better," she explained to Rick, "but he was a rare enjoyer.

"More than once I've heard him say, 'I was prepared to

155

die, Madame Lyons,' " she mimicked his nasal accent outrageously. " 'If I were called to my maker after such a day, I should go with glee—for I had filled it with joyeux to the flowing over.' "

"So this toast is to you young pups. You have filled my joyeux to flowing over, a new lease on pleasure. And life without pleasure is certainly of questionable value!"

I was stunned by what she had said. Stunned but somehow not surprised. I remembered her that night at Prathersville, standing in my grandfather's study, reevoking the essence of his life by bringing her memories to bear on the inanimate articles of that room. It was like Miss Tru to want to give me the joy of another home forever and to endow it with a future, and what remnants of my grandfather still lived in me.

I glanced at Rick and joined him in raising my glass in a small salute as she lifted her own glass to her lips.

We watched as she drained her glass in a single long drink.

"The next toast is mine," Rick cried. "The privilege of being a guest." Then his words trailed off in a shocked expletive.

An explosion of sound filled the room. The great plate-glass window that fronted on the open work deck burst into a million shards of glass. The room was filled with the musical sound of its breaking, but the separate sound that numbed me was the sharp report of a gun—a rifle I would guess.

I looked towards Rick and then Miss Tru. Her head had fallen back against the divan, and her neck, with the cast from the collar-bone brace, was at a strange angle. Through the cracked mass of the plaster a trickle of blood flowed.

"Miss Tru," I cried, leaping towards her.

Her fingers straightened and her wine glass fell, striking the edge of the table and splintering musically in the silence of the room. Then with a strangled cry, her frail body wrenched forward. She was unconscious, her head dangling over the stiff shattered cast like a broken doll.

"My God," Rick hardly glanced at the window before racing to the kitchen phone. I tried to hold Miss Tru's sagging body upright, but her limpness defied me and I was helpless with tears.

I vaguely heard Rick's voice shouting directions on the phone.

"Blankets," Rick shouted to me, "the ambulance is on the way."

After Rick helped me straighten her unconscious form on the divan I turned to him. "Shouldn't you try to find him? Should we go after whoever did this?"

"It's useless," he said flatly. "He could have gone in any direction, and in this fog, a minute is like an hour. Now pull yourself together, Clem, she needs you, not a helpless mess of hysterics."

"But why? Why? Why?" I shouted. He seized my wrists and held them tightly until they hurt.

Almost through his teeth he rebuked me. "That is what this whole madness is about, Clem . . . to find the why. Stay in there. Stay in there."

After my sobs subsided, I went for my jacket and purse. In those few minutes the wailing ambulance had mastered the curves up to the house on the hill. It was followed by a police car whose occupants were out of its doors and into the house before Miss Tru was even loaded on the stretcher.

After a quick exchange of words, Rick and the detectives decided that Rick could bring me behind the ambulance on the way to the hospital. The second policeman was already on the phone by the time we left, barking directions and sending for equipment.

Rick was silent and dark behind the wheel of his car,

guiding it with imprudent speed as we followed the screaming siren of the ambulance down the winding road to Bridgeway and onto Highway 101 north through the streams of
commuter traffic feeding out of the city.

I'll never know how that hospital was able to react so
quickly. Maybe it was by shortwave with the ambulance, but
they were alerted for our arrival and swung into action instantly.

Miss Tru, silent and pale, was wheeled out of our control,
leaving me a shaken mass of uselessness.

"Go wash up with cold water," Rick ordered, pointing
towards the ladies room.

"Pull yourself together hard," he went on. "With luck it
will be a long night."

When I emerged from the rest room, my clothing and
my hands were wet and cold, but I was halfway assembled
again and under some kind of a numb control.

Rick, along with the policeman who had accompanied us,
was waiting for me outside.

"You'd better call that niece of hers, Miss Clement," the
officer advised. "Fortunately the cast slowed down the bullet,
but she is in critical condition at this point."

"The bullet," I said. "They have the bullet?"

"It's already on the way to the lab," he assured me. "But
you better make that call."

I fumbled a coin into the slot and dialed Mel's number.
After the fourth ring, when I was beginning to panic, Bran's
quiet voice finally answered.

"Bran," I said breathlessly. "Thank God. Come to the
emergency room at Marin General. Miss Tru has been shot
. . . she's in critical condition."

"Chrys!" His cry was sheer disbelief. "That can't be! Why
you told me . . ."

"She was okay then, but she was shot . . . through the

window. Oh, please, Bran, don't ask me things, just come and bring Mel. And hurry."

I don't think I even waited for him to answer. I slipped the phone back on its cradle and curled on the tiny bench inside the booth. The ticking had stopped. There was a dead smooth silence in my head. The time had run out. I couldn't even cry, I just sat there a long time hunched over in that little place wishing that the ticking would start again, trying to tell myself that the harried white people beyond the door would succeed in saving her. But the silence inside me gave the lie to my hopes, and I crouched there, helpless.

14

THE END OF
WAITING

If human tragedy has its own private parade ground, then it has to be the emergency room of a hospital. All the color and emotional range of shambling, terrified, inadequate man is in full regalia, exposed without pride, without pretense.

Strength is a burden when it can't be used for anything. Energy becomes a nagging force when immobilized into helpless waiting. Rick sat and rose and walked and sat again. He went to find coffee for me in a paper cup. It tasted a little like vacuum-sweeper dust, but I drank it because it gave me something to do. Around us, small eddies of other lives swirled. One short evening in May had brought together an assortment of people united only by their species and the accident of pain. A child pitifully damaged in a home fire; a very young, very pale boy dragged from the ruins of a speeding motorcycle; an elderly man unconscious from a heart attack. We who waited were an untidy miscellaneous group wholly dependent on those magicians whose masked faces and gloved hands we glimpsed only fleetingly as the doors swung in or out.

They found a room, a small sterile room where Rick and the policeman and I painfully and carefully went over the events of the night again and again. It was strange how the insignificant details of the evening came out one by one. My own problem with memory was with time. I knew that Rick had arrived about five but could only guess that it was five-thirty by the time he had Miss Tru settled on the divan in the living room. There had been that rummaging about for the vase of roses and my nervous checking on the progress of dinner.

Since I had timed the roast to be medium rare at seven-thirty, my best guess was that Miss Tru had called for her precious gift bottle of wine from Rick about seven. From that point on it was sticky. It had taken me a few minutes, maybe five, to get the glasses polished and find the wine-bottle opener.

The policeman noted 7:35 in a strangely round upright script, which seemed uncharacteristic of a man who appeared so quiet . . . it was more an extrovert's type of handwriting, and it distracted me a moment.

"Then what?" he prodded me.

"Then Rick opened the wine," I replied.

Rick shook his head. "No, the phone rang," he corrected me. "I remember that we waited until you got back from the kitchen."

"This was a friendly or a business call?" the officer asked.

"It was Miss Tru's nephew-in-law," I explained, realizing how awkward the phrase sounded. "He was calling from his office in San Francisco to see how Miss Tru had made the trip home from the hospital."

"Still in his office at seven-thirty?" the policeman said.

"That's what he said. He explained that he and his wife were entertaining tonight and implied that he might not get another chance to call."

"And the interval of time between the phone call and the shot?" he asked.

"Three to five minutes at the most," Rick told him. "She made a toast, a little nostalgic speech, and then drank the wine. The bullet struck her chest at about the moment she raised the glass to her lips."

The policeman went to answer a discreet tap on the door. After a whispered conversation he turned back to us, "Miss Lyons' family has arrived. Perhaps you would like to talk to them."

Even in that distracted group, Mel's arrival was dramatic. She had thrown a short coat over an evening dress. The flamboyant dress, white with giant scarlet poppies, swirled its brilliance on the polished hospital floor.

She and Bran had obviously been entertaining quite formally. Bran, in dinner jacket, had rushed her away from their guests to join us. Her face was deadly pale under its patina of makeup. Her eyes seemed to open wide under their tinted lids.

"I've got to go back," Bran said, concern heavy in his voice. "You will take care of her—I'll empty the house and return. I am so sorry, Chrys." He caught my hands and held them tightly. "What happened. Who in the name of God would do such a thing?"

"It's the second attempt on her life in a matter of weeks," Rick pointed out wryly.

"Oh, but that was different," Bran protested. "Breaking

162

and entering, that kind of thing is like fate . . . it strikes indiscriminately."

"The arm of coincidence looks more than long; it looks pretty selectively violent to me," Rick said.

Coincidence. Another conversation intruded between me and their voices. Was it Grand, or was it Miss Tru, who had said, "Call it coincidence, call it fate, call it kismet . . . the Gods still move."

The policeman had left for an interval but now he returned, waiting quietly for Mel and Bran to absorb the first shock of the news.

"I'd like a few minutes with you if possible," he said to them. "Just about her other friends, the situation in the neighborhood."

Rick and I waited alone while the three of them went off to the small room we had left. They returned very quickly and Bran, his arm protective about Mel's stiff body, spoke with exasperation. "I *have* to get back to our guests. It won't take me long once I explain. But take care of her, won't you? I'll be back soon . . . very soon."

Soon is a relative word. But everything was relative that evening. Mel sat between us, but she was only relatively there. She stared silently at the wall and replied to Rick's attempts at conversation in toneless monosyllables.

"She can't die," she said to me once, staring at me bleakly without even seeing me. "She absolutely cannot die!"

Rick twisted his hands between his knees and stared at his shoes. I knew what he must be thinking. I remembered that first night by Miss Tru's fire, when he had told me about Mathew Martin and Vietnam. "Death comes easier than life," he had said that night.

A young intern came to the door and motioned to Rick. They talked in hushed whispers a few moments before he disappeared again. "She's rallying," Rick reported, "but don't build up your hopes. She's old," he paused, "and her life signs aren't that good."

Some time within that hour or two Bran returned. I found myself resenting the firmness of his control, the patience with which he waited, the almost sloppy solicitude he showered on Mel. She didn't seem even to notice him. She stared at the same square of wall as if it contained the answers to all the mysteries that moved about us in that constantly changing waiting room with its low hum of voices, its occasional cries of pain, and the inevitable sound of sirens nearing its doors.

I thought I was ready for whatever came. I wasn't. There was no final sweetness of parting, like that hour I had spent with Grand's hand in mine while morning came to him for the last time. There was nothing personal or private or tender in Miss Tru's death.

Miss Tru had said of Grand that the Gods had loved him to the end. They abandoned her. Surrounded by mechanical marvels and efficient strangers, her heart simply fluttered out of control, and her life fled the thin tortured body it had powered for over sixty years.

"We are sorry," the doctor said. "We did all we could."

I looked at him and turned away. I shrugged off Bran's hand that came out to restrain me. I walked out of that room, down the hall, and into the darkness of the spring night. The outside air smelt of exhaust fumes and pine and vented steam all at once. The sky was black. There were stars, you always know there are stars, but a hidden star might as well not be there at all. I got into Rick's car and curled up on the seat and cried like I hadn't cried since Grand died. They were tears of loss and grief and self-pity, because something that was dear to me had been snatched away, without dignity and without reason.

164

After a while Rick came with Mel, and they got into the car with me.

"Bran has arrangements to make," Rick explained as he put Mel into the car beside me. "We'll take Mel home."

Just as Rick started the motor, the policeman hailed him from the doorway. The motor purred softly as Mel and I sat waiting. They talked quietly and earnestly for what seemed a long time and then Rick nodded and returned to us.

I didn't speak to either of them. I was well past words, and the only thing I could think to say would be unspeakable.

They talked on the way to Mel's house in those hushed tones people use when they have felt death near and seem afraid to startle it into noticing that they still live.

Their words flowed softly past me, half-registering, half-heard. I was too wrapped up in my own absorbing grief.

"I can't conceive of it," Mel repeated stubbornly. "How could anyone hate her so much? What had she done?"

"I came late to this scene," Rick replied quietly. "It exceeds my understanding, but not my anger."

"Just so it isn't like the other," Mel said with sudden ferocity, "just so whoever did it doesn't go scot free."

"It's not likely," Rick said quietly.

"Do you mean they already have a suspect?" I asked.

"It's only a matter of time," Rick said with something like satisfaction. "The first time there was one mistake when the fire didn't catch in time. The killer made his one mistake again."

Mel had been giving quiet directions. Rick followed a winding, wooded road, then turned into a wide horseshoe drive. I thought of the party I had pretended to go to the night the cabby and I had ditched the car that was tailing me.

Suddenly, irrelevantly, I wondered what had happened

to the men who had been following me around. Had I really lost them when I sneaked out of the hotel with Rick bringing my luggage and things? Or was there some other reason that they had been called off my trail?

A massive house loomed over the drive, banked in giant trees. It was Tudor in style, and under the somber angles of its leaded windows, late white camellias glowed in the light of the car.

Rick stopped in front of the massive double-front doors, which were heavily ornamented with brasswork.

"The bullet?" I asked. "Because they got the bullet?"

"Bullets alone aren't that good for evidence I understand," Rick said quietly. "But the killer was on that slatted redwood deck. He evidently wasn't sure he could do the job with the first shot, or maybe he was just absentminded. He kicked the cartridge to reload—or just by habit, who knows. In any event the police found the cartridge in the matted ice plant under the deck. They also have some tire prints from the road below the house, but the cartridge looks promising. It's not from just any old mail-order rifle."

"And they can identify the rifle?" I asked.

"Easy," Rick said confidently. "It was from a 7.61 mm by Sharpe and Hart. There aren't that many of those babies around."

Mel slumped in her seat and covered her face with her hands. The woman at the doorway came down the steps quickly. She was blocky and barrel-shaped in her immaculate black uniform with its lace apron gleaming in the light.

"My dear," I heard her say as she reached for Mel. "My poor, poor dear."

But Mel was weeping inconsolably. "It's my fault," she kept repeating. "It's all my fault!"

Together Rick and the housekeeper led her, a strange bent curve of splashy color, up the stairs and into the house.

166

When Rick returned, his jaw was set hard. He kicked the motor to life and spun around the drive as if the car was the whipping boy for all that had gone wrong that slow, painful evening.

The hands on the dashboard clock stood straight up at twelve as he found his way back onto Sir Francis Drake Boulevard and we started for home.

Some heightened awareness pressed that midnight drive on my mind. Rick, morose and silent, drove slowly, a painful contrast to our harried flight to the hospital just a few hours before. Past the sleeping neighborhoods of Greenbrae and onto the highway, we moved in the sparse traffic of night. Along Bridgeway there was action as always, the sleepless exuberance of the very young, but the hills above town were plastered with darkened houses still with night.

A doe with her dappled faun was grazing on the hill road. She flirted with death to leap in great angled bounds before our car for a few yards before crashing off into the brush and trees.

As the motor died in the carport we heard the faint, slow cry of an owl in the wods beyond the garden, the gentle brushing of its wings in precipitous flight.

I forced myself leadenly out of the car.

The policemen had left, and the house was carefully locked against us and the night. The glass of the huge window that had been shattered by the bullet had been removed, and in its place there was a huge sheet of plywood, cutting most of the view from the room.

A single eye of light winked from the ashes of what had been our festive fire, and an arc of scarlet marked the wine that had flown from Miss Tru's shattered glass.

The bottle of wine with our glasses half-filled still sat on the coffee table.

"Rick," I said slowly. "I think I am going to be sick."

"You're hungry and tired and in shock," he said clinically. "What's your position on hot milk?"

I stared at him stupidly. Mel. I kept hearing Mel's small angry voice crying, "My fault . . . all my fault."

I shook my head. "I don't understand you," I finally said.

"You need to go to bed and you need to sleep," he explained. "I'll fix you hot milk or hot tea or a stiff jolt of whiskey with hot water and lemon. But you're going to drink something hot and pile in."

"Milk," I chose obediently.

I poked restlessly around the kitchen while he warmed the milk. My roast, so carefully timed by the cook-book directions, was a withered knot of charcoal surrounded by dessicated potatoes. The carrots had dwindled to nothing but curved fingers of black in the crust of burned grease.

"Nobody is ever going to confuse you with Julia Child," Rick told me as he handed me the steaming mug of milk.

I grinned at him wanly and inhaled the fragrance of the steam. "I'll settle for an end to all this—for whoever fired that shot."

"Two of us," he said tersely.

Drowsiness spun in my head by the time I had downed the milk. "You realize that I'm staying here tonight?" Rick asked as if it were an accepted fact.

"I'm glad," I said. "There are two more bedrooms downstairs."

"I'm staying here," he informed me. "Right out there on the divan in the living room where I know what is going on."

"I'm in no condition to argue," I admitted.

I could hear his quiet movements in the room beyond as I slipped into Miss Tru's bed. I heard the crackle of fresh logs being fed to the fire. I felt snug and secure and safe. But Miss Tru had felt safe too, I remembered miserably.

I drifted into an uneasy sleep besieged by dreams. There were no words to the dream, only a haunted sense of horror and sound that stopped suddenly, like a voice broken off in midsentence. The dream was bathed in the glint of that red blood wine sparkling in Miss Tru's glass in her final toast.

15

TROLL

From the confused cacophony that stirred in my dream, one sound slowly separated itself and became steady and persistent. It was so persistent that I shook myself to wakefulness to listen tensely. It was like the clink of a grave-digger's shovel striking stone. I shivered and fought back a sudden rush of tears.

It was early. Without looking at the clock I knew it was early. The fog was pale, the way it is when the sun is struggling somewhere behind it. I groped for my robe and pulled myself painfully to my feet. A heaviness in my body made me feel less than human, more like a mechanical body underpowered for its simple needs.

I staggered sleepily down the hall towards the living room. I had forgotten about Rick and was startled to see him, clothes rumpled from sleep, standing at the back window staring down into the garden. When he heard me, he turned and raised his hand to caution me to silence.

I shook my hair back and tiptoed across the room to join him by the sliding doors. Then I understood the sound. Below us in the garden, his slender body covered by some kind of charcoal-gray plastic cape, a figure was bent over a shovel. The click of his shovel in among the roots of the ice plant had been the morbid sound I had wakened to.

"Troll," I explained to Rick in a careful whisper. "My God, Troll doesn't know—"

Rick caught my elbow and looked at me in the strangest way. He didn't speak to me at all. He only laid his long hand flat against the door and forced it open slowly and silently so that he could step out on the deck overlooking the garden.

After only a moment on the deck, Rick leaned over and called down to the laboring figure below him.

"Martin," he called softly. "Mathew Martin."

There was a clatter as the shovel fell from Troll's hand and slid down the incline. He looked up at us from a half-crouching position. His expression of defeated terror made me brace myself against the lintel of the door.

His eyes moved to Rick and quickly all around, as if he felt himself surrounded by unseen enemies. Then with a speed one could never have predicted from his size, he set off running down the slope towards the cover of the eucalyptus, like a man fleeing a thousand demons.

"Mathew," Rick implored, clattering down the fog-dampened steps after him. "Mathew, for God's sake, come back."

But the fleeing figure didn't hesitate or break stride.

Suddenly I couldn't stand it. I ran to the edge of the deck and called out as loudly as I could.

"Troll, come back," I screamed. "We need you. Our witch is dead."

At my words, he skidded to a stop just inside the shadow of the grove. He turned and looked back at me, ignoring Rick who was now almost upon him.

"No," I heard him say quickly and firmly as if to himself. "*No!*"

Then Rick's hand was on his arm, and the two of them stared at each other. I saw Mathew Martin's head drop with an expression of despair. I turned away, suddenly cold and shriveled in my bones with the bleak sense of loss that we all shared.

I watched them climb through the garden together and mount the stairs that same heavy way. Rick was talking, fast and steadily, and so low that I could only catch an occasional word. But his words did not seem to be reaching Mathew Martin. They seemed to slip over the damp surface of that poncho-thing he was wearing, like the moisture from the fog that dripped along his hem. Troll . . . Mathew Martin . . . whoever he was he had somehow, there at the edge of the woods, reached a place where running didn't matter any more . . . nor listening, nor anything.

The open door had chilled the room and I huddled, uncombed and shivering in my robe, as they entered. Mathew stopped mechanically at the door to scrape his boots before he followed Rick in.

"Thank God you came back, Martin," Rick said solidly. "Go make coffee, Clem. We're all going to die of pneumonia."

But Troll caught my eye as I turned. "She didn't die," he said firmly. "She didn't die from that blow . . . she couldn't have!" His voice was angry and defensive, as if I could change the truth with a turn of phrase.

"Not from the blow, Troll," I said slowly. "She was shot last night, through that window that faces the street." As I spoke, Troll seemed to notice the boarded wall for the first time. He stood, his arms limp at his sides, and stared at the blank face of plywood that shut off the view.

I don't know what I expected of him. I guess it had not really registered on me how much self-control the events of a life like his would force on a person. His expression did not change. Only his eyes, as blue as the bay, turned icily hard, as if all human warmth had suddenly left him to drain into the sudden tightening of his fists.

"It was me," he said with a sick finality. "The private doom of Mathew Martin"—he said his name like an expletive—"has destroyed another *good* life."

"Coffee, Clem," Rick said sternly, catching my eye and nodding towards the kitchen. "Nobody makes sense with wet feet."

By the time I returned, they had pulled chairs close to the fire which Rick had built and which was only slowly beginning to crackle to life. I set the tray on the stone ledge of the fireplace. Mathew Martin glanced at me curiously.

"How did you get mixed up in this—a kid like you?"

"I came looking for you," I said, glancing at Rick for support. "I looked for you and found Rick instead."

"A better deal," he said. "Why me?"

"It's an awfully long story," I said lamely. Suddenly my grandfather's debt was such a small thing. As Rick had said so very long ago, a bank vault and a mortuary vault aren't really the same size at all.

"I want to hear your story, Mat," Rick interrupted. "I want to know why you took off running again. I want to know why you shook me off that day downtown. I want to know how you happen to be here, in this place, as a friend of Miss Lyons."

Mathew shook his head and set his untasted mug of coffee down again. "I've gone through this so many times in my mind, trying to figure it out. It was like a series of steps, and the last one went over the edge of a cliff that I didn't know was there.

"Well, I got back," Mathew began again slowly. "It was over, the service hitch was over. I found myself thinking how great it was to have my whole life left in front of me . . ." he slid a quick covert glance at Rick. "You think a lot about the guys who didn't make it when you're out, I discovered."

Rick nodded without speaking.

"Then I remembered that the old thing was still hanging over me," Mat glanced at me, obviously trying to express himself as vaguely as possible. "I decided that I had only half a life unless that mess was cleared up . . . one way or another.

"So I went back to the beginning, to that lousy little town I grew up in. Nobody knew me, I made sure of that. I prowled the newspaper files and read the write-ups of the crime I was supposed to have committed. But there wasn't any crime.

"Yet I knew there was and what had happened."

"And your folks? Did you go see the people who raised you?" Rick asked.

"I cleared it with her, that was all that mattered."

Mathew stopped. Rick waited and poured fresh coffee around.

"Then you decided something," Rick guessed. "What was it?"

"I decided to find my girl," Mathew said stubbornly. "I found out she was married, but I didn't know to whom. I knew she was out here somewhere, and I knew the guy I was looking for was out here too, so I came out and rented that place—you know, the address I sent.

"I got a job, just enough to keep me going and give me time. I knew the guy's name I was looking for, but I hadn't

174

worked out a way to get to him. Then the wildest coincidence in the world hit."

("Call it fate, call it kismet," Miss Tru had said.)

"I was prowling around out in Marin one afternoon and ran into an old lady with a flat tire. I knew her right off. She was a local character."

"Miss Lyons?" Rick asked.

"My witch," Mathew grinned. "She didn't know me from Adam but we hit it off. I didn't know much about her except that she was an aunt of my girl . . . my old girl. So I used her. I really did. All of a sudden the guy didn't seem that important. I wanted to see my girl and talk to her more than anything in the world. So I made friends with my witch. We spent a lot of time together, and although I couldn't really quiz her about anything without tipping her off, I did get some questions in and some answers.

"She told me her niece was married to some rich guy with a big place over here in Marin. That she didn't think she'd ever been happy since an accident had killed her dad. What a funny marriage she had—they even had separate wings of the house and stuff like that."

He glanced about at the room. "This got to be a second home to me, or maybe a first one. I'd come mornings and work the garden a little and shout up to her when I thought we both needed breakfast. And she used to take me to a hill she liked. She said it was her niece's favorite place too, and I'd probably run into her there sooner or later.

"So that's where I spent my time, working my night shift down on Union Street, having breakfast with Miss Lyons and haunting that hill . . . just in case."

"And it worked?" Rick asked.

Mathew nodded, staring down at the rug and wringing his hands.

"Yeah, it worked. Look how great it worked."

175

"There's more," Rick nudged.

"Too much more," Mathew said quietly. He looked at me straight. "I'd adopted her, you see," he mused suddenly. "There was a sharp clean edge to her that I liked. I told myself that if I had a family she'd be in it somewhere—sharp and bright and level as an alfalfa field."

I suddenly leaned forward and laid my hand on Mathew Martin's arm.

"Mat," I said carefully, "I'm from Prathersville too, sort of." His glance was defensive and startled, but I steadied my hand on him. "I want you to tell us why you left in the first place."

"It's dead now," he said flatly. "All dead."

"We don't think so," Rick said firmly. "Even if it is, we want to know, just for the book."

The book. Suddenly I heard Miss Tru's voice. In that locked closet downstairs were her journals. There was a chance—just an outside chance. The key. I had the key somewhere. It must be in the pocket of my beige velvet blazer. I had been wearing that blazer when Rick came. I had worn it all through the vigil at the hospital, and it was lying on the floor of the bathroom right now where I had peeled off everything and dropped them in my sick exhaustion of the night before.

But I didn't move. Mathew Martin stirred to his feet and said with sudden irritation, "Doesn't anybody here have a cigarette?"

"There are some in the freezer," I said, remembering seeing them when I put away groceries. When I got back and handed him the pack he stared at them curiously. "I bet that my old witch kept them here for . . ." he paused, "her niece. That's her brand too.

"Prathersville was a lot of lifetimes ago," he said slowly. "I was there until my senior year was about to begin." He

176

hesitated and then went on painfully. "I was real gone on a girl, and she was on me. We'd seen a lot of each other. I wanted to get engaged, but she was afraid to ask her dad—afraid he'd think she was too young—so we just went steady. But we both knew how it was.

"I was working in the hay fields east of town for a guy with a big spread. We worked late that night, and it was about seven when I came back through town towards home. When I passed the mill, I saw her father's car parked outside with the workers all gone.

"I'd been waiting for a chance like that, to talk to him by himself, tell him how it was between her and me, but I'd never had the break before. I parked my jalopy out on the street. I remember thinking it might make a bad impression if he saw that junk pile I was driving.

"When I walked into the mill, I knew right off he wasn't alone. I heard voices, men's voices, shouting. Then there was fighting and the sound of furniture falling. I was scared, but I headed for the office anyway. I only saw the silhouettes through that glazed glass they use on office doors, but I saw this guy throw a helluva punch and the other man go down.

"I hit the door with my shoulder but it was locked. Then I really bulled in there and knocked that door through. When I got inside, this man was standing there, just standing there, smiling at me. I didn't even know the guy except that he worked for the old man. My girl's dad was lying in a pool of blood on the floor with a gash in his head where the corner of the desk had gone in.

"I must have stood staring like a bumpkin for a long minute because this guy moved behind me to the door. He was cool . . . the coolest cat I've ever seen.

" 'That was a real show,' he said quietly. 'Coming in here out of the hayfields and taking on a man like Ambrose Lyons.

177

So now he's dead, the old man is dead, and you're in real trouble, son.'

"I stammered something and started for him, but he was too quick. He was outside that door and down those stairs before I could get near him.

"We had one of those chases, those wild chases in that big storeroom downstairs with the hay bales stacked along the wall and machines dripping oil and a thousand shadows big enough to hide a man. I thought I had him, a sound behind me kind of. But when I turned it wasn't a movement at all, it was fire. He had tossed a match or lighter or something in that dry hay heap and the flames were licking up like pillars.

"When I turned, the big doors had been slammed shut and locked. I was in there, that was all, with the fire taking the place fast and Mr. Lyons dead upstairs in his office. I flailed around, my head full of smoke and not able to think straight. Then I thought I could hear, over the sound of the fires, the screams of sirens coming out from town. I could hardly breathe, but I climbed on one of those machines and made a flying jump at a high window. I was cut something all to hell from the glass and bruised all over from the fall but I was out.

"I gathered myself up in a panic, coughing and aching and blood all over me. My car parked there for everyone to see and me in the shape I was and the old man dead and the place burning down. Everybody in town knew about his girl and me."

Mathew fell silent and spread out his hands. "What does a bastard kid from the wrong side of the tracks do when he's caught in a frame like that?"

"Run," Rick said quietly. "Run like hell."

"And don't think it hasn't been," Mathew commented drily.

I was stunned. I had been listening to Mathew's story, mentally fingering the key in my blazer pocket, itching to get that journal, to see what Miss Tru had written as an entry at that time. But suddenly the whole picture was askew. Suddenly there was the extra piece. Ambrose Lyons had not died—he had been murdered. Did Mel know that? Where *was* Mel in all of this?

"Excuse me, Troll," I said suddenly. "Did you ever meet your girl on that hill?"

He didn't meet my eyes. "I did," he said flatly.

"And you told her this story?"

He nodded. "But she didn't believe it. She went all to pieces and sobbed in my arms for a long time, but she didn't really believe me."

"She had another story?" Rick asked.

"That's the strangest part," Mathew said thoughtfully. "She said she never thought it was an accident. She had known all the time that her dad was murdered, but she also knew it was me that did it. But you see the newspapers never called it anything else. There must have been a rumor or something, but my Mom hadn't heard it. It was strange and scary the way she couldn't face either fact . . . that I'd done it or that I hadn't. It was hell."

"But why were you running?" Rick asked. "Why were you running that last time we met?"

"Because I went to the man. I finally located him, and I waited for him in his parking garage downtown. I was way upstairs where there was nobody else around. I waited and I confronted him with it. I threatened to expose him. I told him he had to confess to only one person what had actually happened, or I'd kill him.

"He sneered at me like before. 'The police, I suppose?' and he taunted me about being crazy.

179

"I told him the only person wasn't any cop, it was a girl —a girl named Mel."

I don't think that Mathew even saw the quick glance that Rick and I exchanged.

"He went for me," Mathew went on, "I think I might have killed him there, only a car came down the ramp and caught us in the headlights. There he was in his hand-tailored silk suit and all the credentials and me in service castoffs and no way to defend myself. The car stopped and the guy jumped out yelling. I took off . . . running again.

"But he found where I was. He meant to kill me. He said it, and he meant it, and he had all the cards—the money, the prestige—and I had nothing but speed on him."

"And your girl. Did you see her after that?" Rick asked.

"Only once," Mathew said. "She was being tailed and she was scared stiff and she didn't know of what. That's when I faded. But I couldn't stay away from here. I came at dawn before anyone was ever around, and I didn't figure that he could ever link me with old Miss Lyons. That's how come I caught the fire that morning. Whoever set it hadn't been gone an hour, but I saw the smoke through the windows and turned the alarm in."

The jangle of the phone broke into my thoughts. Rick started for it, then stopped and grinned . . . "Maybe for the sake of your reputation you better catch that, Clem."

I caught it on the third ring. It was only seven o'clock but there was no apology from Bran North. He asked briskly, "Is Mel there?" in a sudden tense spurting of words.

"No," I said, startled by the urgency of his tone. "She's not here."

"You're sure?" he said almost angrily. "She hasn't *been* there?"

"We left her at home last night, at your house," I explained. "The housekeeper was there. Wasn't she there when you got in?"

"I don't know," his voice was hard with tension. "Her door was closed and the lights out. I figured she was asleep and didn't need to be bothered. I just slept in, but when I got up a while ago, she was gone."

"Was her car there last night?" I asked.

"I don't know," he said defeatedly. "I didn't even open the garage, just parked in the drive and went in to bed. It had been a long day," he reminded me.

"But where could she be?" I asked, getting a little frightened myself, remembering how frantic she had been when we left her.

Somehow in the course of our conversation he had gotten control of himself. His voice grew calmer, almost cold with control.

"Don't worry, Chrys. I'll find her. I think maybe I know where she might be."

Both Mathew and Rick were watching me as I replaced the receiver.

"Mel is gone," I told Rick. "Bran doesn't even know when she left because he got in late and didn't disturb her. He just presumed she was here with me."

"But where could she be?" Rick asked.

Slowly, like the unwinding of a great spring, Mathew had risen to his feet.

"Mel?" he asked quietly. "Mel is gone?"

I nodded. "That was her husband Brandon North . . . he stayed at the hospital after—"

"Brandon North?" Mat spit the name out like a curse. I nodded.

Rick was staring at Mathew with a puzzled frown.

"So what's he going to do?" Mathew's voice was menacing.

"He says he knows where she must be," I explained.

"I know too," Mathew said coldly. "Let's go."

"But . . . Mat," I resisted.

"Slap something on, Clem," Rick said quietly. "Fast."

Mathew was hunched in the back seat of Rick's car when I skidded out to the carport in a pair of slacks and a jacket. My hair was still uncombed, but the impatient racing of Rick's motor made that seem inconsequential.

Mathew gave terse directions and urged indecent speed on Rick as we tore down the hill and onto Bridgeway towards the underpass to the west.

That trip was like riding in a car with a bomb at your back. Mathew's tension was a viable force behind me in the speeding car with tires screaming on the curves towards the headlands. His voice was quiet and menacing from the backseat.

"I never knew who she married. I never asked. She never told me. It was just Mel again, after so long."

"And that name means something?" Rick asked mildly, cornering at a speed well beyond the manufacturer's recommendations.

"Brandon North is the guy who killed her father," Mathew said through clenched teeth. "He was the guy who set fire to the mill and taught me to run."

16

THE HIGH PLACE

The fog grew thick as we rose towards the headlands. I gripped the seat as Rick sped up the curves following the same road that Mel had taken me on that afternoon when we talked. The place seemed vastly different now. It was cold and bleak, and the wind carried a rolling thunder of sound from the trafficway and the bridge beneath us. My cheeks ached with cold as we rose into the density of fog and barreled towards the sea.

The twin towers of the Golden Gate Bridge rose from behind the landmass only to disappear into the heavy fog like disembodied red giants. The city existed only as a vague shadow, spire and pyramid, rectangle and tower, fusing into a chiaroscuro silhouette.

Rick swung the car in a quick semicircle to catch a spot

in the small parking area against the fence. Both of the North cars were there, Mel's silver Jaguar with its top down and the seat gleaming from condensed moisture. The sleek Citroen that Bran drove was parked beside it, its hood steaming slightly in the cold air.

"This was her place too," I told Rick compulsively. "Miss Tru's place."

He laid his hand on my arm lightly as he glanced back at Mathew who was already out of the car with a light spring.

Once on the ground Mat stared through the mist indecisively, as if he did not know where to start his search.

The various fog horns of the bay were speaking and answering in low moans through the mist. We started through the fence that separated the road from the battlements. The visibility was dropping so steadily that only the first set of bunkers were clear; behind that lay only the whiteness of thickened air with its overload of muted sound.

Something low and prickly grew along the slopes. The bushes were tufted as if with miniature cotton, and the stuff clung to me as I made my way along the path.

The icy wind pressed against us as we crossed the old tunneled battlement area toward the bunkers beyond. I caught at Rick's arm, stumbling on the rough ground, and my face burned with cold and the whipping of the wind.

Mathew pressed slightly before us, almost disappearing into the mist. We followed him, moving towards the sea. The crisp tang of salt was heavier in the air and the wind stronger with every step forward.

Above and beyond us lay the sea. I could see vaguely through the mist the bent trees that leaned landward. Up there was the point. It was the point that Mel had taken me to—her "high place."

Scrambling among the slippery stones and gripping the

nettles of bushes for help, we rose to that high plateau. A
strange hush fell on me up there. It was as if the sound was
cowering below in that more protected place. The wind was
unsteady here, gusting and pushing by turns, so that my balance was uncertain. I clutched my raincoat tighter and
tightened my arms against my chest.

Suddenly, at a swerving of the mist, I thought I saw a
figure there on the edge of the point.

"Mel," I cried out with relief. "Mel, it's me, Chrys."

When she didn't answer, I had a moment of terror that
maybe she would jump, maybe that was what she had come
up here to do. I remembered Miss Tru's concern about this
place and her saying that Mel didn't need anyone else to
harm her.

Strangely enough, Rick and Mathew by some silent agreement hung back together, probably to keep from startling
Mel.

I ran breathlessly toward the silent figure and was literally
upon it when I realized that it was too solid a figure for Mel
and too tall. Bran turned to me in the mist, with a strange
cold smile on his face, emptied now of charm, just a controlled smile as if he were immensely satisfied with himself.

"So you knew too," he said quietly. "You knew where Mel
would come in the end."

As he turned, I realized that there on that edge of the
precipice he was holding Mel in a death grip, her eyes wide
with terror above his hand that covered her mouth to keep
her from answering, from screaming for help.

"No, Bran, No!" I shouted. "Let her go."

Now the mist hid the precipice beneath us, but I remembered its rocky incline, the sharp drop onto that small semicircle of sand where the gulls had clustered in a small jostling
congregation.

"She betrayed me," he said bitterly. "She destroyed her-

185

self. She had no right . . . no right to betray me, no right to destroy herself. She belonged to me."

I listened, struggling with my own agony and something strange about his words that didn't seem to fit right.

"That boy," he said slowly. "That filthy bastard boy, he was the one who did it. He took away what was mine."

"Bran, you aren't being rational," I cried. "Mathew, Rick, help!"

Bran had not looked past me into the glowering mist with its twisted trees. He had not realized that I was not alone. His expression of terrified horror confirmed that he had no reason to believe that I had not come alone. After all, I had answered the phone, he had no way to know that there had been three of us in that room when his frantic call came.

"Get back," he hissed. "Get back, all of you. This is my affair—my world."

Tears were streaming down my face and I ached with the chill of the wind pressing against me.

"Help, Rick, help!" I screamed.

But Brandon North had no eyes for Rick. The figure that moved towards him was not Rick.

Mathew Martin moved like a gaunt wraith in the trailing mist, his beard and the huge rubber poncho swirling about him in the wind. His eyes, beneath the mat of hair, were terrifying even to me.

"Go back," Bran said, his voice rising. "Leave us alone. Go back."

Mathew didn't speak. He didn't even seem to hear. He walked across the open place that lay between them slowly, almost ponderously, his hands clenched lightly at his side. His eyes never left Bran's face.

"I'll throw her. I'll throw her down," Bran threatened in a screech, struggling with Mel to turn her towards the brink.

186

Mathew Martin finally spoke into the trailing mist. The wind whipped the words from his mouth giving them an unreal and eerie sound.

"Let her go," he said quietly.

"Murderer," Bran screamed. "You killed old man Lyons, and now you've killed Mel."

"Let her go," Mathew spoke again, not slowing his pace, but nearing them with every step like a mountain moving inexorably toward the sea.

"One more step," Bran screeched. "One more step and I'll throw her down."

Overhead I heard the sweetness of something brushing, a circle of gulls were so low that the sounds of their flight filled my head.

Then suddenly, Mathew stopped. He was so near that had Mel been able to get her arms free she could have reached out and touched him. He stopped dead still and towered there in the mist with his eyes fast on Bran's frantic face.

I was immobilized by terror. Like Bran, I watched Mat's tall slender figure with its cape whipping like something demonic. I didn't even think of Rick in those moments of fascinated terror.

Then everything happened at once. There seemed to be no sequence of movements. It was as if the two men moved in an easy flow of strength, like the graceful curl of a whip swaying toward Bran and Mel. Rick dived for Mel, catching her firmly a little below the waist and rolling quickly backwards over the stones and harsh abutments away from the sea. Bran struggled as he clung to her. From a low crouch, Mathew caught the angle of Bran's jaw, throwing his head backwards, loosening his grip on Mel so that, as Bran struggled for balance on that cliff's edge, Rick and Mel rolled free, and I could hear the low thrumming rhythm of Mel's hysterical sobs behind us.

187

But Bran was no easy mark as he fought for balance. Mathew seized him by the coat front, struggling to hold him from the abyss below. I could hear the rent of the fabric giving under Bran's weight. I saw Mathew's frantic clutching to save him from the fall. It was useless. The only sound was a thin fading scream as Bran fell into the mist below.

The air seemed suddenly full of birds. The flutter of a thousand gulls beat the air about us as we stood transfixed in a cloud of white wings. The birds rose and circled and pipped and screamed with insult as Rick ran to my side and I clung to him. We went to the edge and stared down into the fog below.

I was conscious of the hysterical dysrhythmic sobs coming from my throat above the sounds of the gulls and the muffled roar of the bridge traffic.

A trail of mist cleared, and far, far below us I saw that same narrow crescent of sand. A legion of gulls fluttered between us and the crumpled body of Brandon North there on that small stretch of beach. The sea lace swayed tentatively towards his outspread arms. He was staring upwards sightlessly at the sky while the sea nudged him curiously.

Even as I stared, a little ill and weak from shock, the gulls began to settle down again.

They settled back slowly on their narrow strip of rock-sheltered sand, as if no intruder had come. Ignoring the remnant of what had been a man, they lit on their small sacred territory, jockeying each other for position, exploring troublesome lice under a wing, and tucking up a single leg they turned their scarlet tipped beaks steadily towards the pounding sea.

I pulled my eyes from the horrifying scene below to see Mel folded like something small and frail and wounded in the voluminous folds of Mathew Martin's cloak. Her head was buried in his chest as if to shut out all sight and sound of a world that was past her bearing.

From above the medley of sounds on the hill we could distinguish a new rhythm, the rise and fall of police sirens. We saw the scarlet blinkers working their way along the traffic below and stood waiting, the four of us, at the top of the world—at the end of the world for Bran. For the first time, Mathew Martin was not running.

17

THE KEY

Morning was almost gone when we finally left the hilltop. There were pictures and measurements and endless technical things that had to be done when the second wave of police arrived.

"He was trying to kill me," Mel explained. "It was either him or me. Mathew had no choice."

After taking the sedative that the housekeeper had insisted on, Mel had pretended to go to bed. But she waited until the housekeeper was back in her own quarters and went to Bran's study.

"The gun was gone," she said simply. "The Sharpe and Hart was gone. And I knew I just couldn't stay there any more. I had to get away and think. You see, I had tried so hard not to believe . . . not to believe that Bran had really done all those things. . . ."

"All what things?" the policeman broke in quietly.

"My father," she said in a stiff small voice. "A long time ago my father was killed in a fire at our mill. It was put off as an accident, but Bran, my husband, had always told me that another man had done it."

"And your husband concealed the crime?" the policeman asked curiously. "Why?"

"Because the man he said killed my dad was the boy I was in love with. He did it to shelter me, he said, and I believed him." She paused. "Then there was my aunt. I was seeing a man, another man. I heard my aunt and Bran talking one night, fighting really. He accused her of meddling; he threatened her, and she threatened him with something too . . . something about the mill fire again.

"That night her house was invaded and set on fire, and somebody tried to kill her with a blow on the head.

"And then there was the gun. He bragged a lot about that gun. There's something special about it. It hasn't been made for a long time. It was originally from abroad; the parts were Swedish I think maybe, or French. But he used to brag that there weren't a half dozen like it on the West Coast.

"To think," she said helplessly. "I needed to think . . ." The policeman held her gaze and she dropped her eyes. ". . . and maybe die."

"And then your husband came here?" the policeman asked.

She nodded, staring down at her hands. "He came up there on the hill where I was standing trying to get my courage up," she paused.

"He was very gentle with me," she said with surprise. "At first he was very gentle, very solicitous as he always was. He asked me why I had come, and I told him I needed to think.

" 'Not to meet anyone?' " he had asked.

"I shook my head because I couldn't get words to come out. I was cold. I'd been there so long, since a little after midnight. And I was sick. Sick at the dying, my father . . . Aunt Tru.

"Suddenly he flew into a rage. 'You came here to meet *him*,' he accused me. 'You think he can come and save you, don't you? That bastard from the wrong side of the tracks who killed your father?'

" 'He didn't kill my father,' I screamed. 'You did. I know you did. It makes sense that way and it never did the other way. Mathew wouldn't do that. He'd never do that.'

"That's when he grabbed me and started shaking me. He called me every filthy name in the world, accused Aunt Tru of getting Mathew and me together. He admitted he'd tried to kill her and finally done it because, as he said, 'She was the only one who knew . . . who could prove anything.' "

"How did he figure she could prove anything about that old crime?" the policeman asked curiously.

Melanie trembled, shaking her head.

"The journals," I said suddenly. "It would all be in the journals. Miss Tru . . . Miss Lyons kept a daily journal all her life. There must have been something in that journal, or Bran thought there was, that would bring up all that old scene."

We heard the shouted cries of the men in the boats that fought the tide to retrieve Bran's body from its ring of gulls. We finally were taken downtown where Rick and I separately and exhaustively were questioned about the struggle, the ensuing fight and Bran's fall.

Rick and I were both able to identify the private detectives who had shadowed me and only been mysteriously withdrawn after I moved out to Sausalito. They had nothing to hide, they claimed. In their business capacity they had been hired by Brandon North to find Mathew Martin. Bran himself had dismissed them from following me after I left the St. Francis. He told them he could take care of it himself from then on.

There would be more questioning. There would be a hearing. But the truth had emerged like the headlands from the fog as day progressed.

By midafternoon, Mel's eyes were wide and dark with fatigue, and Rick took us both home, to Miss Tru's. "I can't ever go back to that house of Bran's," Mel said flatly. "Not ever."

"What about you, Mat?" Mel asked. "You won't go away . . . promise me you won't go away again."

"I couldn't right now if I wanted to," he smiled. "And I don't want to. But Clem and you both look awful. Get some rest. We'll be in touch."

Melanie slipped from the shower right into bed but I could not settle down. It was already five o'clock in Prathersville so I called Mr. McAllister at home.

"Technically I can't open that box without your key, Chrys," he said. "But you could get it here by air mail special delivery probably tomorrow." He harumphed in that banker way, then added, "I could manage to have that parcel for you to pick up at any bank you name in San Francisco before noon on Monday."

"Monday it is," I thanked him. "Oh, and if you see Vinnie, tell her I *will* write . . . I haven't forgotten really."

I hadn't forgotten Vinnie. Maybe she didn't have the time to teach me to cook but she had taught me other, less happy things. As soon as the key was dispatched to Mr. McAllister, I went through the careful ritual of death that I had seen her perform after Grand died.

193

After I told Mel's housekeeper of Bran's death (in an accident), I told her that Mel would be in charge of the arrangements and that she could be reached at my house.

Actually I made the decisions and arrangements alone. I cancelled without compunction the funeral arrangements Bran had made for Miss Tru.

Brandon North would be buried in the grave he had selected for her, the last victim of his possessive murderous passion for his wife . . . a place that was far from the town that had spawned this whole ugly tragedy.

Miss Tru would make one last trip home. In the coffin with her, there would be a single laurel wreath, a twin to the one I had set on Grand's folded hands those months before. She would lie in the Maxwell plot in Prathersville next to the only man she ever loved.

When that was finished I did what I had been waiting to do since that afternoon that Miss Tru first came home flushed with happiness to begin a new life with me. I went downstairs and unlocked the closet that held the journals. "August, 1959" was on the third shelf. Some day I would read them all. Some day I would follow the pattern of Miss Tru's life from that first journal, dated January, 1920, clear through to that last entry she had been making the afternoon before she died. But for now it was August, 1959, that I wanted to read.

Prathersville came back to me with a rush of nostalgia as I read through the entries. The careful flowing script recorded such a miscellany of things . . . the sulphuring of the hybrid tea roses and a colloquy between herself and the butcher on the scarcity of lamb in his store. Leafing through the month I noticed an almost-empty page.

The small entry was heartbreaking. It read simply.

Ambrose, my only brother is dead. He expired in a

fire that destroyed his mill. I find myself peering back through time as through muddied water, trying to remember that Ambrose was once a child of scarred knees and small square body, that his sweetness of boyhood was the basis of his fineness as a man. I grieve for him. I grieve for Melanie who loved him as I do. I am lonelier this day.

I shook my head with disbelief. That couldn't be all. There was nothing there to suggest foul play in the fire, there was nothing to indicate that Mathew was at all involved. This was Miss Tru withdrawing even from her own words in the loneliness of her grief.

I flipped a page backwards and read the entry of the previous day.

Jackson came by to see me this afternoon. We sat where the sun makes long angles on the veranda floor, turning the straightness of the boards into a pattern of light and dark. We talked of Chryseis and Sylvia's recent wedding. We talked of local things. We talked of Mel and how she flowers as a woman. Then something strange happened that I do not quite understand. I told him, laughingly, of how Melanie is being courted by men of all ages—this stunning boy from nowhere who squires her about town and makes her glow with beauty, and how Brandon North has been sulking and dithering ever since she lost her head over her young schoolmate.

'You jest about this," he almost commanded me.

"Certainly not," I told him as sharply. "Bran North has been after that girl since she was a child. He adores her. But what can come of it?"

He rose suddenly, which is not Jackson's way, and said curtly, "Nothing must come of it. I will see to that myself. Your brother will be at the mill if I stopped by?"

"Of course," I said. "Whatever has gotten into you?"

"The fox knows many things, Tru," he said almost apologetically. "I am the hedgehog who knows only one *big* thing."

He marched off down the walk like a crusader into battle. I must remember to ask Ambrose about that conversation. Jackson is as strange as he is unique.

There was a curious, letdown feeling. There ought to be more. I couldn't accept this entry as the whole of her response to the tragedy of her brother's death.

Idly I flipped through the entries after her brother's death. The pattern had changed. There was the same weather report, the details of what she was reading, her frustration at a painting that wasn't shaping up the way she had conceived it, but in among those ordinary entries were small ruminations, almost musings that showed that her mind was dwelling on the fire and its consequences.

It wasn't like Ambrose to be unconscious of the starting of that fire until it was out of control. He had too firm a notion of the hazards of that business and that building.

What happened to those fire extinguishers that he had bought at such cost and placed around the mill—the one by his desk and the one hooked to the ladder by the stairs? Why didn't he get to use them? How could he have been trapped like that?

Jackson's visit keeps coming back to me. He hasn't mentioned anything about it again, but he had been there with Brose that afternoon. He had some strong reason to talk to Brose. I keep remembering what Jackson said before he left, 'This hedgehog knows one big thing.' Is it possible that something Jackson told Brose *caused* that accident? I am growing irrational. How could that be? But something urges me to the thought and I watch the change in Melanie with sadness. What did Jackson know, and was it somehow dangerous to Ambrose?

I was still there with the journal open on my lap as the room darkened and the lights winked on across the bay. So that was the final key. Something known to my grandfather and shared with Ambrose Lyons had precipitated the quarrel that led to Ambrose's death. How right Rick had been about the long lines that knitted the tragedies together!

I heard Mel stirring in the other room. She wandered out sleepily, almost lost in the voluminous folds of my robe. She made herself a scotch and soda and curled by the fire, watching the smoke from her cigarette trail lazily towards the beamed ceiling.

"How can I feel so at peace, Chrys?" she asked quietly. "I have no pain, no remorse, no guilt about Bran, just peace."

"Because the mills of the Gods have ground slowly, but they have ground exceedingly small," I said almost sulkily.

She stared at me. "I don't understand you," she said.

"I don't even understand myself," I admitted smiling at her. "When Mathew left Prathersville after the fire, why did you think he had gone?"

She looked away from me into the fire.

"Brandon told me that Mathew had been the one who started the fire, that he had really killed Daddy because Daddy wouldn't let us be engaged."

"Did you believe it?"

"Not at first," she admitted. "But Mat didn't come back. He didn't ever come back, and Bran was so gentle . . . he cared so much."

"But then when Mathew told you his side of the story, you couldn't believe that either?"

She stared at me in astonishment. Then, as if my knowing exceeded her understanding, she writhed a little. "My God, Chrys, try to think on how it is to have been married to a man all that time . . . and to have been faced by that choice."

197

"The thing that strikes me as the biggest coincidence of all is that you and Mathew ever got together again after all these years. I know he came out here looking for you, but he didn't even know your married name and he never found it out from Miss Tru either. It was a wild and unbelievable chance that you ever connected."

"It wasn't really chance, Chrys," she said quietly. "You see, I sort of hid a part of me. You remember how we always had to do with Mamma? I did that with Bran too. I hid a part of myself from Bran . . . the part that still loved Mathew, in spite of everything."

"I looked for him, Chrys." She stared at me with those wide-set lovely eyes that always have seemed magical to me. "I looked for him in little side streets in France on holiday, I watched for him at Christmas celebrations in Mexico City; in every crowd, in every man's face, I have searched for Mathew all this time."

"And then you found him?"

"I think he found *me*," she said quietly. "You know Aunt Tru and I both love ships. We used to go together to watch Bran's ships go out to sea, always to that same place." Her voice broke. "That point above the bridge near Kirby Cove."

I nodded.

"One day when I was feeling all locked in, the way I sometimes get, Aunt Tru called. She suggested that I drive up to the knoll and meet her. 'If I don't get there right off, wait for me,' she added. 'I have an errand on the way and might be delayed.'

"I was there for a while, maybe half an hour, but I didn't mind waiting. I was watching the ships and the skyline and the swaying of the gulls.

"Then suddenly I realized that someone was coming and I turned, expecting it to be Aunt Tru. I was startled to see that it was a man, because I expected her on that great old cane of hers. But even as I watched the man come I somehow wasn't afraid. There was something in his walk and the way he carried himself that was familiar.

"I just stood there and waited for him to get to where I was. We looked at each other for a long time, and then he took me in his arms and it was as if all the time had been stripped away and we were kids again and happy.

"Finally we pulled apart and he grinned at me, that funny grin of his.

" 'How did you know to find me, Mathew?' I asked him.

" 'A witch sent me,' he kidded softly and took me in his arms again."

She caught her knees in her arms and hugged them like a child and stared into the fire. "We were so happy, Chrys . . . so completely happy. But I had to be so careful. I know the housekeeper listens in on every telephone conversation I have. I complained to Bran, but he said I imagined it and anyway, what was I going to say that was secret?" She shrugged. "That was why I got so scared the night you called. I knew she was going to tell him right off that you were out here to find Mathew.

"We met there a lot," she went on. "Finally I realized that Bran knew something was different. Then we got very secret about our meetings. I used to feel like we were being followed all the time, but I didn't ever tell Mathew for fear he would go away again."

"Were you afraid of Bran?"

"Not until then," she said slowly. "Once he was angry about a man at a party and he said hard things. He said he would see me dead before he lost me, but I thought maybe all men acted that way with their wives.

"But then one day I actually saw the detective. It wasn't a feeling any more; I saw him. I was so scared that I refused

199

to meet Mat again. It was right about then that Aunt Tru's house was broken into and she was nearly killed. I was terrified. I couldn't believe it was Bran, but there had been that fight between them the night before and threats. . . ."

"Bran could have done that without your knowing it?"

"Too easy," she admitted. "We have separate wings of the house. I got pettish about it a long time ago, having no privacy and all. He could have left after bringing me home and done it and been home and everything normal by breakfast. I thought about it then and fought the idea and remembered what Mat had said about the fire. I nearly lost my mind those weeks. And then you came."

"And I called and asked about Mathew on the phone. Some brains."

"How were you to know?" she reassured me, touching me gently on the knee. "But after that call from you, everything did get stranger."

"I got a note from you and Bran at that hotel that night," I told her, "and somebody followed me after that . . . followed me everywhere I went."

She stared at me and shivered.

"You know that it was Miss Tru who sent Mathew to you on the hill, don't you, Mel? You know they were friends and he always called her the Witch . . . it was a joke between them.

She stared at me. "No, no, he never told me that. I didn't even know they knew each other."

"She always had funny friends," I reminded her.

Suddenly she buried her face in her hands. "It's all my fault, Chrys. Aunt Tru died because of me."

"That's backwards," I said crossly. "You can't be held accountable for Bran's madness."

"But Aunt Tru, why Aunt Tru?"

"Women and elephants," I told her wryly. "Do you

remember the night that she got angry at you and said you were losing your mind?"

Mel stared at me, "She told you about that?"

"She did," I nodded. "She made a journal entry on it. She did threaten Bran about the fire while you were in the bathroom. That night she was attacked, you know that."

"Oh Chrys, Chrys," she moaned, shivering into her own arms. "It just goes on and on and on. What point is there to it anyway?"

"Mathew," I said firmly. "Miss Tru's troll and your Mathew."

I recognized Rick's car roaring into the drive and heard its rumbling stop. I was already on my feet before I caught Mel's funny little angled grin.

"Just Mathew," she said quietly. "Just Mathew, that's all."

Mel stayed with me at Miss Tru's over that Saturday. We sat together at the small memorial service for Miss Tru, and then the strange hypocritical service that was Brandon North's last rites.

As we left Bran's graveside in the glittering sunlight, Mel turned to me.

"Now I can go home again," she said simply. "I can go home now and stay there."

"You know where you are welcome," I reminded her.

She nodded. "And I'll at least see you Monday . . . at noon?"

"Monday at noon," I said.

I watched her walk to the waiting car.

Her dark hair blended into the slender fit of her dark coat, and there was straightness to her back that seemed almost defiant. She turned and looked back at me, and the impression of defensive childishness vanished. Somewhere inside of Mel, beneath and beyond the dark power of her eyes, lay a strength that reassured me.

18

THE FINAL DOOR

It was late Monday morning when the call came from the bank that the package from Mr. McAllister had arrived and was there for me to pick up. Rick watched with quiet amusement as I went through the stiff little ostrich dance of identification and witnessing of signatures that preceded their handing over the sealed packet that I had first seen back in March in that special bank vault.

Out in the car I held the package in my lap and stared at it. A real sense of depression settled over me at the physical presence of that strangely shaped parcel. The first day I had seen the package came back with force—the turgid sky over Prathersville, the voluble little old spinster at the bank, but most of all my encounter with the hostile man at Corners

West, and the subsequent poignancy of his wife's call at my home.

I tried to picture Mathew Martin in that setting, the ramshackle old store and those people. He didn't fit. Alas, he wouldn't come alive to me as Mathew Martin of Corners West at all. I doubted that he ever would.

To me he was Troll, the slender giant in the garden of Miss Tru's house, her good funny friend who had spent companionable hours by her fireside over coffee. Troll was the man who had saved her life after Bran's first attempt. Troll was the terrifying figure emerging from the swirling mist to deliver Mel from Bran's vengeance at the high place above Kirby Cove.

Troll was what Mathew Martin had become in years of running; Troll had been the secret shadow behind my grandfather's eyes.

Now, with the packet ready to be delivered to him at noon, I had finally reached the end of the search that had begun so quietly that March morning.

And now it was all over. Miss Tru's pointless death agonies were at least explained, if Bran's reasons could be accepted as explanation.

I huddled deep into my coat, into the bucket seat beside Rick as if by withdrawing physically I could escape the horrors of the days just past. Rick stolidly maneuvered the car north towards Sausalito. The Sienna maidens of the Palace of Arts and Sciences stared sightlessly back at me as we passed. Once we got onto the bridge, the traffic slowed, sorting itself into chosen lanes. I wouldn't look. I wouldn't even glance at that point of the headlands above Kirby Cove. It was etched more bitterly in my mind than my eyes could grasp anyway.

But the swaying gulls still hung above that place. Even without looking, they flashed in my peripheral vision, floating above the inlet, jostling, settling, rising and swaying again in the wind currents.

They had always been there, I told myself. They had been there when Drake passed this bay going north, unconscious of the inland sea that lay shrouded in the fog.

The fog lay like a bar of light along the horizon hiding the Farallones and the open sea beyond. It was coming just as it had come the day that Miss Tru was murdered. The wind that was bringing it whipped against the car so that Rick's hands tightened on the wheel.

"Maybe you should talk to me," I told Rick in a small tight voice.

Rick's glance was quick and unsmiling. "You don't want to tell me what you are thinking?"

"I don't have any words of my own," I confessed. "Like my grandfather, my head is too stuffed with other people's words."

"Bran's?," he asked. "Mel's? or Miss Tru's?"

"Nothing so modern," I confessed. "A Greek poet from Rhegium, a man called Ibycus."

"I'd probably prefer Ibycus to the moderns at this point," he invited. "Share."

As always, the words came into my mind in my grandfather's voice. They even moved from my lips with his pacing, the slow measured tones, weighted with his love of the lines.

"For me Love sleeps at no season," I recited.

"But like the north wind from Thrace aflame with Lightening / It comes with a rush from the Cyprian, dark and shameless / With shrivelling madness." My voice faltered and stopped.

"Dark and shameless with shrivelling madness," Rick repeated softly.

"I'm shriveled," I explained after a minute. "That's why

204

it keeps coming back. I'm shriveled by it all. By Bran's incredible self-delusions, by what they were doing to Mel, and Mathew Martin's long suffering."

The dark of the tunnel was sudden and quieting. Rick caught my hand and pressed it tight for a minute.

"And I think it scares me a little," I admitted in the darkness of the tunnel. "It scares me that nothing ever changes inside of man."

"All the old tragedies keep being replayed again. The temples are artifacts and the cranes are diminished to gulls, but the old Gods hold their sway over man."

"Well," he said quietly. "It is almost over now. Nothing will bring back Mel's father or Miss Tru, but once you hand Mathew that package, the circle will be complete and the Gods will be satisfied. Have you thought of how it might have ended out here if your grandfather had not set that search for you, Clem?"

"Oh, I don't know," I replied cynically. "Probably it would all have bled off into time, another unsolved murder, Mel destroyed by her forced hypocrisy, and Mat an eternal fugitive."

He shook his head. "Not on your life," he said positively. "It would have blown up some way, and not too prettily when it went."

"He'll come, won't he?" I asked Rick as the car moved through the thinning traffic along Bridgeway. "Mathew will come today?"

"He'll come," Rick said. "He'll come because he told you he would, if for no other reason."

"Like what reason?" I asked.

"Because Mel will be there," he said simply. "He'll come just to see for himself that she's all right."

"Can anything work out for them . . . after all this?" I asked.

"That's a very chancy question," he said turning off onto the hill road. "They're both pretty badly wounded. But if they can heal together, they'll be knit for good."

"One of your guests came early," Rick said quietly as he swung up the drive towards the carport. Mel's little silver Jaguar was parked in the extra slot. As Rick pulled in behind the Chevy, I watched Mel turn to look at us. She was changed. The wind had loosened her usually immaculate hair so that it was tossed about the upturned collar of her coat. Without makeup, not even the small color of lipstick, she looked like a cold abandoned child.

She shivered as she got out of the car. "I couldn't stand it at home," she admitted. "So I waited here."

"But how long?" Rick asked crossly. She looked frozen to the bone and trembly on her feet.

"Awhile," she said evasively, "maybe an hour."

I put my arm around her. "We'll defrost you fast!"

She wandered about aimlessly while Rick stacked fire logs and I made coffee.

"I hope he comes," I said nervously as the bell in the hall chimed the half hour. "He's got to come, you know."

"He'll come," Mel said quietly. "He told me he would come."

"Where has he stayed all this time, Mel?" I asked. "How has he both been hidden and yet always here when Miss Tru needed him?"

"Funny places," she said slowly. "There's a commune in Mill Valley where he stays part of the time. He carries his weight there with money for food and things. There's a houseboat in Sausalito that he caretakes sometimes when the owner goes off sailing. They are 'Mathew' kind of places . . . hidden places."

"But he doesn't have to hide anymore," Rick reminded us.

Mel's small face was tight with a frown. "You have to learn *not* to hide after a while, just like you have to learn to hide in the first place."

Rick heard him first, the cat quickness of his tread on the deck stairs from the garden. I realized at Mat's almost wincing glance around the room that maybe of all of us, Mathew missed Tru the most. Then his glance caught Mel's, and he looked at her a long minute before going to sit by her. He seemed careful not to touch her as she sat tightly beside him on the divan, as if she were crystal that was likely to explode on contact.

"I don't really understand why we are all here," he said finally, looking questioningly at Rick. "It's all over now isn't it? Except for the police wrap-ups."

"Not quite," I said. "I have something that belongs to you that I promised to deliver to you."

He studied me, expressionlessly. "Do you think anything can make any difference now?"

"I don't know," I admitted. "I only know that it was the dying wish of my grandfather that you be found, and this was in a safety deposit box for you."

I handed him the packet which he turned in his hands curiously.

"Would you like to take it off into the other room by yourself?" Rick asked suddenly.

"Maybe so," Mathew decided slowly. "Maybe I'd rather do that."

"I have an even better idea," I said. "Mathew, you stay here, and Mel and Rick will help me fix some sandwiches. I'm the world's least-expert kitchen help, but they are hopeless braggarts about themselves. I can point to things and they can do the clever parts."

The three of us were conspicuously noisy in that kitchen. Rick and Mel had a lively controversy about whether Basque buns were better filled with wedges of ham and cheese or dressed tuna and cheese. They did agree on thirty minutes in the oven at 350 degrees. (I was allowed to preheat the oven, that being considered the extent of my skill.)

Rick insisted on making warmed-up baked beans. He rummaged for brown sugar and dry mustard and catsup and seemed to slosh them indiscriminately into the pan with the beans.

"Much better with crisped bacon bits on top," Mel sniffed haughtily, "but probably a passable performance."

Our consciousness of Mat's silence in the room beyond forced us into a strained jocularity. The mood was such a change from the days past that it seemed almost hysteric to me as I stood a little apart from it and listened.

"Do you seriously think I should become involved with a girl who can't even make decent coffee?" Rick asked Mel as if I weren't there.

"You could always live in one of her houses where she wasn't," Mel pointed out. "There are a lot of good places to eat between Indiana and Sausalito if you are commuting."

"A girl of property is very picky about who she lets court her," I said to them. "I may just pick out a playmate for his cooking ability."

"I accept," Rick cried jubilantly, waving a slotted spoon at me. "In front of a witness, I accept."

Suddenly Mel's frozen silence caught both Rick's attention and my own.

Mathew was standing in the doorway with the strangest expression on his face. He was looking at me as if he and I were the only people in the world, much less in that room.

"Chryseis?" he asked slowly.

"Yes," I replied, caught off guard by the strangeness of his tone, and by the use of my whole name.

"You are Chryseis?" he said firmly.

"I am Chryseis," I said quietly, leaning without thinking against the support of Rick's arm suddenly behind me.

"Not Clem, not Chrys, but Chryseis?"

I nodded silently. Mel's large eyes moved from Mat to me, and she waited with that incredible tenseness that she had somehow learned in her years of being someone else for Bran.

"Can you tell me who or what Alastor is?"

I stared a moment and the wheels spun. Like a school child repeating a familiar phrase by rote, I parroted, "Alastor was a Nemesis—the evil genius of a house. He was the avenging power who visited the sins of the father upon their children."

I glanced down at Mathew's hands. He was holding folded sheets of the parchment that my grandfather used for all his personal correspondence. The level italic lines of Grand's lovely script ran endlessly, it seemed to me, across those pages that hung loosely at Mat's side.

"Do you know what was in that parcel, Chryseis?" he asked, his voice sounding strange and formal in its use of my name.

I shook my head. "The seals were never broken until you did it," I pointed out.

He handed me the letter, then turned away. He passed through the doorway and then looked back. "All of you," he shook his head almost distractedly, "I think you need to read it . . . all of you." Then he was gone.

Mel instinctively followed him and Rick and I were right behind her. We watched as he walked like a sleeping man across the deck and down the stairs, then slumped at the bottom, like a confused child, staring off through the eucalyptus and past the mounds of nodding marguerites to the fog-draped bay beyond.

Rick and Mel turned to me as I slid into a dining-room

chair. I think I lost consciousness that they were there as I read the long letter aloud to them.

August 14, 1969
Prathersville, Indiana

From: Jackson Lane Maxwell
To: Mathew
> the foster child raised by Cecil and Rhoda Martin of the following address: Martin's Store, Corners West, Prathersville, Indiana

My dear Mathew:

This letter is written in the fervent hope that it need never be delivered. What I have to say to you is something that I pray to the Gods I may have the opportunity to say to you personally, man to man.

But since, for the last ten years, you have been lost to me, and I have been unable, despite diligent search, to locate your whereabouts, I feel the need to cleanse myself of my great guilt and confess to you the blindness of my misuse of you, even if this confession reach you after my death.

I pray that you might realize that the world has changed in the time of your maturing, and that, slowly, I have changed with it.

My child, Sylvia Maxwell, conceived a child out of wedlock when she was a schoolgirl of sixteen. Unprepared as I was for any imperfection in this child who had been the whole of my life since her mother's death many years before, I reacted with anger and blame to all who surrounded me. The boy who was the father of the child denied his paternity of the unborn baby and retaliated to my accusations with threats of destroying her reputation in this town which bears her family name on its every landmark.

I removed her from the town, arranged for her confinement in a refuge in the East, and at birth her son was taken from her. In my attempt (mistaken, I am now

210

sure) to give her a chance to begin her life anew, she was told that the child did not live.

My daughter, your mother, finished her education in the East, was married, divorced, and was remarried before her premature death.

In order that I might be near you and have some knowledge of your care and well-being, I had you placed with the above family in Prathersville. I arranged for them to have a generous allowance for your upbringing and that upon maturity you would have available ample funds for whatever education or business you wished to pursue.

But then, in the fall of 1959, you disappeared. I had only the most unsupported rumor to aid my understanding in your fleeing your home.

As the years have passed, I have gradually liquidated various assets and accrued investments in your name. If this letter comes to you after my death it will be accompanied with documents that provide you with an estate of equal value to that inherited by your half sister, Chryseis Maxwell Clement, my daughter's only other living heir.

Your sister Chryseis knows nothing of your existence. She knows nothing of what I now consider your mother's human weakness. At the expense of great heartbreak on my own part, as I cherish her dearly, I have kept your sister removed from this town so that she might be as little as possible infected by shadows of this past, and in the hope that no gossip or slander destroy for her her mother's name.

I cannot in any fairness ask forgiveness for my failure to openly acknowledge your life and take you into the family you belonged to at birth. I can only ask that you understand my weakness and believe in the purity of my intent.

At birth I gave you the name of Mathew, electing to use

211

the Gaelic rather than English spelling because of your father's predominantly Irish descent. I truly believed that your birth was for me, as it is stated in the last five words of the Gospel of Matthew, "the end of the world." I was wrong. The world goes on, your life goes on, and the life of your sister Chryseis will go on into the time beyond my time.

So with these properties, I do also endow to you the name I denied you. You may keep the name of Martin, now understanding its source; but I would be honored if you chose to use Maxwell which is the name you deserve, or, if you should desire, you might use the name of North, since the man who sired and denied you was named Brandon North.

I would quote to you from the poet Alcaeus, "'Tis said that wrath is the last thing in a man to grow old." I have outlived my wrath and most of my dreams.

Only one dream remains, that the Gods look kindly on your life and protect you from Alastor.

Jackson Lane Maxwell

When my reading stopped, we were all silent for a moment, then Rick sighed and said quietly, "Great Gods, what a masterful old man."

I was suddenly weak. It was as if the flood of words from those parchment sheets had washed away concealed layers of my understanding. Things that had never made sense to me were suddenly crystal clear—my grandfather's determined abandonment of me to private schools when I wanted so much to be there at home with him, the strange way I could communicate with him about my own mother only from some great emotional distance as if she were a dream person whose reality he couldn't evoke. It even made clear why he had sold off his great estate piece by piece until his world was roped in by its ancient hedge of lilacs. It was poignant to realize that he had broken the silence of his personal tragedy to warn Ambrose Lyons about Brandon North and that Ambrose had died in the subsequent argument, all to protect Mel. And I understood why Mel's marriage was kept a secret from me until she and Bran had left the area for good.

Most of all, I could understand why Grand should have lain awake in his solitary bed and grieved for this lost grandson of his who might never be privy to the truth of his own beginnings, nor inherit the property that was my grandfather's real debt to him.

I was conscious of Mel rising. I glanced at her and saw that scarlet spots of color had risen in her cheeks. With a briskness of step that was very uncharacteristic of her, she crossed the room. We heard the quick tapping of her descent as she joined Mathew on the stairs in the garden. Rick and I watched as she sat down beside him, looking very small and fragile. The sleeve of her coat slid across his back as she laid her head against his shoulder.

Into the silence a small bell began to ring from the kitchen. Rick grinned at me crookedly and went to get the sandwiches out of the oven.

"Clem," he said thoughtfully, "we have just lived through the longest thirty minutes in the life of any man."

"Or any woman," I agreed, pulling his bean pot off the flame just as it began to crackle drily.

Maybe one of the forty-seven things I like best about Rick is the way he divides the extraordinary into ordinary-sized pieces that I can handle emotionally. He walked to the sliding doors and called down to the still figures on the stairs below.

"Come and get it," he shouted irreverently, "before we throw it out."

I have forgotten who won the argument about the filling

for the Basque buns, but they were steaming and delicious. The baked beans were spicy and fabulous in spite of their haphazard seasoning. The cold wine was from a gallon jug without distinction but it tasted like nectar to all of us.

We ate, carefully skirting the huge change that each of us had undergone at the reading of that letter. Only one of us could bring that subject back to words again, and finally he did.

Mathew's eyes were like the bay on a clear day as he looked across the table at me and smiled.

"Tell me, Sister Chryseis," he said pedantically, "Is there some Greek story that runs like this—that a child be hidden and his father try to destroy him and in the end the father dies by the son's hand for love of his father's wife?"

"Mathew!" Mel cried in reproach.

"There is another and better story, Brother Mathew," I echoed his phrasing. "And Melanie knows it as well as I."

"I know such a story, Chrys?" she asked suddenly confused.

I nodded. "Remember how you told me of the white birds on that cliff above Kirby Cove?"

She nodded, her eyes dropping from mine.

"And how they reminded you of my grandfather's painting of the Cranes of Ibycus?"

She nodded again and looked at me searchingly. "And what that story meant . . . what it proved?" I went on.

I waited for her to search her mind. I watched her eyes widen as the words came back to her slowly, out of the long ago, in that same unforgettable sequence that they had been stamped on my own memory. "When all other human means of justice fail, the Gods themselves will see that justice is done."

The wind was rising the way it does in early afternoon. The branches of the eucalyptus swayed their fragrance against

214

the wall of that aerie and we were all silent. Somehow, in between the voice of the rising wind and the tick of the clock in the hall, I could hear a door closing gently off somewhere in a quieter world.

And I knew that behind that door there lurked no specters, only the peace of an old man sleeping beneath a wreath of well-earned laurel.

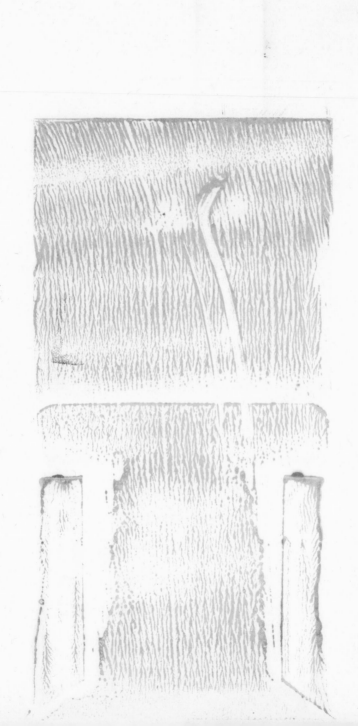